J. F. Richmond

Diamonds

Unpolished and Polished

J. F. Richmond

Diamonds
Unpolished and Polished

ISBN/EAN: 9783741123153

Manufactured in Europe, USA, Canada, Australia, Japa

Cover: Foto ©Andreas Hilbeck / pixelio.de

Manufactured and distributed by brebook publishing software
(www.brebook.com)

J. F. Richmond

Diamonds

DIAMONDS,

Unpolished and Polished,

By Rev. J. F. RICHMOND,

AUTHOR OF "NEW YORK AND ITS INSTITUTIONS."

If man is not rising upward to be an angel, he is sinking downward to be a devil. He cannot stop at the beast.

COLERIDGE.

ILLUSTRATED.

NEW YORK:

NELSON & PHILLIPS.

CINCINNATI:

HITCHCOCK & WALDEN,

1873.

Diamond Gulch.

PREFACE.

MAN occupies the foremost rank among terrestrial tribes, and is strangely linked to all the past and to every thing yet to come. Nothing beneath is to him unimportant, while above stretches a chain of golden links lost only in the heights of Infinitude. His fertile nature he is called to study and cultivate. One has well said: "Those advantages peculiar to man seem to have been furnished him in view of his moral and intellectual natures. Among these Religion and Science stand forth with greatest prominence; the first adapted to his moral, the second to his intellectual constitution. These two natures of man are intimately blended in their origin, and should keep pace with each other in their development. He who neglects the cultivation of his moral feelings circumscribes the exercise of his intellect. He who neglects the intellect will be a dwarf in religion. He who cultivates both will by this means facilitate the improvement of each, and may shine both in the world of intellect and of morals."

All minds are attracted by the beautiful, the brilliant, and what they esteem valuable. The untutored savage listens attentively to the roar of the cataract and the storm, and sees beauty in the crystal, the sunset, and the cloud. Civilized man revels in the esthetic, and is proud of his substantial accumulations. He searches the domain of earth to find its beauties and luxuries, and harrows its sides for its enduring treasures. If man could be made to see that there are beauties transcending the landscape, the arch, the pyramid; pleasures surpassing those of sense; gold more valuable than that of Ophir and California; diamonds outshining the products of Golconda and Peru; if he could be made to feel that in himself the Creator has concentrated more of wealth than the material universe contains—that he is an epitome of nature, of time, and of eternity—a great point in his elevation would be secured. In the hope of in some measure inculcating this great lesson this volume has been prepared.   J. F. RICHMOND.

MOUNT KISCO, N. Y., *March* 1, 1873.

CONTENTS.

CHAPTER IV.

POLISHING ROUGH DIAMONDS.

CHAPTER V.

BRILLIANTS.

CHAPTER VI.

DIAMONDS OF THE FIRST WATER.

CHAPTER VII.

SECLUDED JEWELS.

CHAPTER VIII.

VALUE OF THE DIAMOND.

CHAPTER IX.

LOST DIAMONDS.

CHAPTER X.

HOW TO PRESERVE JEWELS.

Illustrations.

DIAMONDS,

UNPOLISHED AND POLISHED.

CHAPTER I.

PRECIOUS STONES.

THROUGH her mines nature furnishes a variety of hard and showy substances which have in all ages attracted attention among the curious, the wealthy, and the scientific. Had these precious stones existed in sufficient abundance the great could have erected courtly palaces that would have survived the waste of unnumbered years ; but with most of the varieties the supply is so limited that they must ever remain little else than objects of curiosity. Nearly all precious stones are transparent or translucent, and are formed of simple elements of nature or of inorganic compounds, crystallized. They probably once existed in a fluid state, and solidified by gradual processes. Their inward structure presents a series of thin plates, or coats, one over the other, similar to metallic substances which were once fluid. Many of them are characterized by a variety of brilliant colors, which may have been imparted by some mineral substance or earthly exhalation while in their hardening state, before their lamina were closed. This appears the more probable because many colored gems are found in close proximity to metallic veins, and from the fact that they often lose their color when long subjected to the influence of intense heat.

With all the ancient nations precious stones constituted an important part of their wealth, and were an essential and highly-prized ornament of distinguished persons, particularly of kings. The ancient Egyptians possessed stores of this kind of treasure, and at the present time precious stones are often exhumed from the mummy-pits and cemeteries of that interesting people.

In the early literature of Greece we find numerous traces of precious stones. Homer speaks of the shining gems in the ear-rings of

Juno. Plato believed that precious stones were produced by the vivifying spirit abiding in the stars, and at a later period a common notion prevailed that some rare stones possessed the power of generating others. From these and other theories taught by their most learned men, the Greeks attributed nearly every variety of magic to precious stones.

"When the Romans conquered Greece and Egypt they took home with them the taste for precious stones, and carried it to a stupendous pitch, the opulent and patrician classes vieing with each other in the extravagant use of jewels. Cæsar is said to have paid a sum equal to two hundred and fifty thousand dollars for a single pearl. In later periods of Roman history we find numberless instances of the estimation in which jewels were held. In the time of the Ptolemies the Egyptians used them in profusion for ornamenting arms, drinking-cups, and the altars of the gods. Caligula is said to have adorned his horse with a collar of pearls ; the shoes of Heliogabalus were studded with gems, and the statues of the gods had eyes of precious stones." Gems and rare stones are mentioned in the mythology of the Hindoos ;

they have been found in the buried ruins of Herculaneum and Pompeii; they were also found by the Spaniards in the possession of the native Mexicans and Peruvians in America. We therefore conclude that all heathen nations, and nearly all classes of persons, have highly prized them.

The ancient Hebrews held them in high esteem, as we learn from numerous allusions and paragraphs of Old Testament history. The breastplate of the high-priest, worn on public occasions, was a rich and ingeniously wrought ornament, containing twelve precious stones, appropriately inscribed, set in gold. Precious stones glistened in the diadem of their kings; they were set in rings and worn by wealthy noblemen, and made a matter of traffic by the merchants. They were obtained chiefly from India and Arabia. The Queen of Sheba brought presents to Solomon of "spices, gold, and precious stones." The navy of Hiram, king of Tyre, "brought gold from Ophir," and also "precious stones." How many varieties were then known we shall not attempt to decide. Job mentions nine, including the crystal, the coral, and the pearl. The breastplate of the high priest contained twelve, and twelve are also mentioned by St. John as foundations in the walls of the New Jerusalem. Several of those mentioned, however, are of the same stone, (chalcedony,) differing simply in their shades of coloring ; and some others may be grouped together, two and two, as identical, except in their variations of color. The list, however, comprises most of the precious stones of modern times, and, we may suppose, of the world.

For the benefit of the youthful reader, and such as have not given the subject particular attention, we insert a partial list of the precious stones, with some account of their qualities and uses.

The JASPER is a variety of opaque, impure quartz, of red, yellow, or other dull color, but capable of high polish. It was wrought by the ancients into numerous gems and ornaments, and it is still used in making vases, seals, and snuff-boxes.

The SAPPHIRE is pure crystallized alumina, and is the second hardest substance in nature. It is a blue, transparent crystal. Inferior varieties of sapphire are found in many places in the

2

United States.   When this stone is not of a
blue color it is known by other names.   The
bright-red sapphire is known as the *oriental
ruby*, and is a gem of great beauty and value.
The largest ever known was brought from
China, and was some years ago placed in the
imperial crown of Russia.   When the sapphire
is yellow it is known as *oriental topaz;* when
green, as *oriental emerald;* when violet, as *oriental amethyst;* and when hair-brown, as *ada-
mantine spar.*   The *common ruby* is a variety
of the spinel.

The CHALCEDONY is a translucent, massive
variety of quartz, usually of a pale-grayish,
blueish, or light-brown shade, and has a luster
resembling wax.   The stalactites in caves are
icicles of chalcedony hanging from the roof of
the cavern.   *Agate* is a variety of chalcedony
with different colors arranged in stripes or
layers, and sometimes contains spots in ground
colors, and even figures.

The CARNELIAN, identical with sardius and
sardonyx, is a silicious, flesh-colored, semi-
transparent gem, akin to the chalcedony.   It is
much used in common jewelry in all countries,
and by the Japanese in making beads.

The CHRYSOPRASE is a translucent, flinty quartz of an apple-green or greenish-golden color, and is sometimes spotted. It is green-colored chalcedony, with very little luster. Some of the ancients believed it contained the power of healing disease.

The ONYX is another variety of the chalcedony, consisting of parallel layers of different shades of color, and is much used in making cameos. A grayish-red chalcedony is known as *sard*. There is also a greenish-gray translucent chalcedony, obtained from Ceylon and Malabar, called *cat's eye*, which is a gem of considerable value.

The CHRYSOLITE, composed of silica, magnesia, and iron, is found generally in prismatic form, varying in color from pale-green to bottle-green, and sometimes of a yellow or of a wine color, and at times colorless. Mineralogists now suppose the topaz of the ancients to be identical with the chrysolite of the moderns.

The EMERALD is a green or bluish-green six-sided prism, composed of silica, alumina, and glucina. It is identical with the *beryl*, except differing slightly in color. The finest emeralds come from Grenada ; large and coarse specimens are also found in Siberia. The finest beryls are obtained from Hindustan and Brazil.

The JACINTH is a species of *zircon*, a hard, transparent, hyacinthine stone composed of zirconia and silica. The *hyacinth* is red, and the other varieties are brown or gray, and sometimes shading into yellow. The jacinth is believed to be identical with the ancient *ligure*.

The AMETHYST is usually transparent quartz, of a violet-blue color, found in six-sided crystalline form, and sometimes in pebble shape. The specimens obtained from India were most prized by the ancients. Some of inferior quality were also obtained from Arabia and Syria. They believed this stone a preservative against the power of intoxication.

The CARBUNCLE is composed of silica, alumina, and lime, with oxide of iron, and is consequently a deep red-colored gem, with a mixture of scarlet. The Greeks called it *anthrax*, on account of its resemblance to a live coal. It is usually found pure in an angular form, and when held between the eye and the sun it exactly resembles a burning coal. This gem is identical with the modern *garnet*, which is found in a variety of colors.

The OPAL is composed chiefly of silex, and is found in three varieties : the *precious opal* exhibits a peculiar play of delicate tints ; the *fire opal* is less transparent, with colors like the red and yellow of flame ; the *common opal* exhibits a kind of milky appearance.

The TOURMALINE is a three-sided or six-sided prism, terminated by three-sided pyramids. It is found in colors of black, brown, blue, green, and red.

We should, perhaps, add to these the PEARL, which is a gem formed by nature in the shells of several species of mollusks, particularly the pearl oyster. It is obtained from the bed of rivers and the sea at various places in Asia, Europe, and America. The pearl is composed of the carbonate of lime interstratified with animal membranes. It is of a hard, smooth, lustrous substance, and of a silvery or bluish-white color.

The natives of Ceylon carry on an extensive business in the pearl fisheries, and are probably the most dexterous men in the world engaged in this perilous business. They can remain under water several minutes without breathing, and can handle a rope and pick up the smallest objects with their toes as well we can with our fingers.

But of all the precious stones and minerals of the world the DIAMOND is the hardest, most brilliant, and valuable. It was for many ages supposed to be indestructible by fire, or any other element or agency known to man. It is not acted upon by acids or alkalies, and if protected from the action of the atmosphere may be heated to whiteness without injury. Modern chemistry has, however, ascertained that if exposed to the air at a temperature a little below that required to melt silver, it is burned or dissipated in the form of carbonic acid gas. In substance it is carbon in its purest and most perfect state of crystallization. The perfect form of this crystal, and that into which many are converted by cleavage, is that of two four-sided pyramids joined at their bases, (octahedron.) The faces of many of these gems when found are rounded, presenting a convex surface, and the edges are often curved. Diamonds are found in a variety of colors, as well as colorless and perfectly transparent. The latter are most esteemed, and, on account of their resemblance to pure water, are styled "diamonds of the first water." Some are tinted like the rose, and if transparent, these are much prized. Next to the rose a green-colored diamond is considered most valuable. A yellow, an orange, a cinnamon, a blue, or a black, is less esteemed.

At precisely what period the diamond was first discovered, or where it came to be first prized, is not now easy to ascertain. The term diamond occurs in our English translation of the Bible four times — twice in the book of Exodus, once in Jeremiah, and once in Ezekiel; but whether the original Hebrew word (yahalom) in Exodus or (shamir) in Jeremiah signified the gem now recognized as the diamond, or the jasper, the onyx, the emerald, or some other variety of hard, brilliant stone, is a matter over which critics have greatly differed, and about which no one can be entirely certain. It is extremely doubtful whether the diamond was known in the days of Moses, and, on account of the difficulty of engraving it, whether it could have been used in the breastplate of the high-priest. It was long known in Asia before it was discovered in any other quarter of the globe; and the celebrated diamond known as the *Koh-i-noor*, or " Mountain of Light," owned by the Queen of England, is said to have a well-defined history running back beyond the Christian era. The art of cutting and polishing diamonds probably originated in Asia at an early period, but it was not introduced into Europe until about the middle of the fifteenth century.

Properly speaking, no diamond mines have ever been discovered. The gems are found in alluvial deposits, scattered among pebbles, and often associated with gold. They have drifted from their original homes, and often lie exposed on the banks of rivers. One of the most valuable diamonds found in the United States was picked up by a laborer, in 1856, on the banks of the James River, opposite the city of Richmond. Sometimes they are found buried twenty or thirty feet in the soil, concealed by half a dozen distinct alluvial strata, as in the island of Borneo.

The famous diamond fields of Golconda in Hindustan seem to have furnished for many years all the diamonds of the world. The gems were not as large as some specimens since obtained in other countries, but excelled in hardness and brilliancy. These mines have become unproductive, and are now generally abandoned.

Rich diamonds have been obtained from the island of Borneo, the largest of which fell into the hands of the Sultan of Mattan, and weighs three hundred and sixty-seven carats. It is valued at several million dollars. Diamonds have been found also in Bengal, in the gold regions of Siberia, and a few in Georgia, North Carolina, and Virginia. A new excitement has sprung up in our country during the present year (1872) in relation to the discovery of diamonds on the Rio Colorado, Chiquito River, California. A company has recently been organized with a capital of ten million dollars, and many rich gems are already reported to have been found, one of which weighs over one hundred carats. If the field is half as rich as reported, the United States, already famous in the abundance of their mineral harvests, will be still more distinguished.*

About 1730 the celebrated diamond field at Serro do Frio, in Brazil, was discovered. The region was known as a gold district, and slaves were compelled to search for that metal. They occasionally found bright stones, which were for the most part thrown away. At length

* This mine has since proved an ingenious swindle.

some one, more curious than the rest, preserved a few, and showed them to the governor-
general of the mines, who had previously spent
some time in the East Indies. He suspected
that they were diamonds. The Portuguese government sent a minister to Holland with specimens to ascertain their real value, and, after
bearing a critical test, they were pronounced
very fine diamonds. A new interest was suddenly manifested toward Brazil. The Portuguese government dispatched the Rio Janeiro
fleet in search of the precious gems, and in
1732 it returned with eleven hundred and forty-
six ounces, which so overstocked the market as
to nearly ruin the old dealers of Europe. From
1730 to 1814 there was an average yield of
thirty-six thousand carats per annum. It has
since been much increased. From ten thousand to twenty thousand persons have for many
years found employment and subsistence around
these diamond fields, which have been worked
by government and by private parties and com-
panies for one hundred and forty-two years, and
are still productive. The gems are found in a
species of gravel, which is dug up and taken to
a shed for washing. Through the center of this

shed a stream of water is conducted, on one side of which is placed a number of sloping troughs about three feet wide, communicating with the stream at one end. About a bushel of this gravel is placed in a trough, the water let on to carry away the mud, the large stones are thrown out, after which the search for the diamonds begins. When this work was performed by slaves an overseer was stationed near by to watch them and receive the gems. It was the custom to liberate a slave who found a diamond weighing seventeen and a half carats.

A Brazilian slave was one day searching in the bed of a river for gems, and with an iron bar broke through a crust of silicious materials cemented by oxide of iron, and discovered a bed of diamonds worth fifteen hundred thousand dollars. They were carried to England, and the market was again so overstocked that many diamond merchants were ruined. The Brazilian diamond " Estrella do Sul " was sold for one hundred and eighty thousand dollars ; another, the " Star of the South," imported to France about fifteen years ago, weighed in its rough state two hundred and fifty-four and a

half carats ; another, held by the King of Portugal, was at one time valued at twenty-eight
million dollars.   It weighs about eighteen hundred carats, but the genuineness of the stone
has been questioned.

In 1869, diamonds were discovered on the bank
of the Vaal River in South Africa.   In 1870, a
large gem, subsequently known as the " Star of
South Africa," was brought into the market,
and has since been cut into a handsome stone.
It is now the property of the Prince of Wales,
and is valued at thirty thousand pounds sterling.   The introduction of this valuable gem
into the civilized world produced intense excitement among treasure-seekers, and many
thousands have flocked to South Africa in
search of diamonds.   The Vaal River flows
through a vast sandy, stony, hilly, barren tract
of country, till recently but little inhabited.
Mines are now worked at different points for
more than one hundred miles along the course
of the river, and across a belt fully fifty miles
wide.   New places are being almost weekly
reported.   Many of the diamonds have been
found on the copays, and along the banks of
the ancient beds of the river.   If the mine is at

Work at Sorting-Table in Diamond Diggings.

a distance from the river the gravel and earth are conveyed to its banks, or the water for washing is carried to the mine. If water is taken to the mine it is placed in large tubs, and the gravel having been dried in the sun and sifted, is taken up in a sieve and washed from one tub to another until the earth disappears, when the residue is spread upon a table for minute examination.

At the river-bank the gravel is washed in a box about three feet long and two feet deep, open at the top and at one end near the bottom, and supplied with rockers like the cradle of a child. In this cradle are placed two or three sieves several inches apart, the finest being at the bottom to retain the small stones of value. After placing half a bushel of gravel in the upper sieve one man pours on water while another seizes the perpendicular handle of the cradle and rocks it violently, continuing until the fine stones can be easily discovered. The sorting is done with great rapidity by experienced miners. An inexperienced miner will be elated with many beautiful crystals, but will soon find that they are wholly valueless. The real gem is not easily overlooked. " One will seem to stare at you," says a gentleman who has spent some time at the diamond field, "like a brilliant eye from among its dark, lusterless associates. After once picking up a diamond among the gravel the digger will have no hesitancy in deciding what are and what are not these beautiful gems with as much certainty as in any case where two things are in question."

By what silent processes the great Architect elaborates so exquisite a gem from such an unsightly substance as charcoal, and transforms the blackest specimen of matter into the most transparent and brilliant, is a mystery that all the students of nature have been unable to solve. In India the diamond is found associated with the new red sandstone, in Brazil with talcose schist. It belongs manifestly to the metamorphic group of rocks which yield gold, but to what particular rock none has yet been able to tell. If the carbon of which it is composed was ever distributed in the vegetable kingdom, by what means it was collected, and whether it came from the earth's surface, or was exhaled from internal carbonic vaults locked up for ages in the calcareous rocks, or secreted from vast collections of fossilized plants, is what no geologist has been able to ascertain. Composed of a single substance abundant in nature, the matter of its production appears simple, yet so mysterious are the processes of its formation that all the researches of time shed no real light on this interesting problem. Next to the philosopher's stone, the manufacture of genuine diamonds has offered the most lucrative incentives to the ingenious chemist ; but though many eminent scholars have bent their energies in this direction, and have repeatedly produced other and more complicated forms in mineralogy, they have one and all utterly failed to solidify carbon into a diamond, and, after most protracted and painstaking experiments, have been compelled to exclaim with the defeated magicians of Egypt, " *Surely this is the finger of God !* "

CHAPTER II.

BURIED DIAMONDS.

HE diamond is far from being the most useful substance in nature. Copper, lead, tin, platina, iron, silver, gold, quicksilver, and salt are each turned to many more useful accounts. The gross but useful metals are immensely more important to civilized society than those denominated "precious." Without the former we should have little convenience, culture, or happiness. We could neither plow, nor dig, nor prune, nor graft, nor mow, nor reap, nor weave, nor print, nor build, nor carry on, as we now do, any of the arts of civilization. We could have no convenient vehicle of travel, no steamboat, rail-car, or telegraph; no foundries, factories, or temples; little commerce, little progress. How intimately are these things connected with all we value and with every thing in the world either good or great!

The diamond, however, has its uses. It is sometimes made into lenses for small microscopes ; its fragments, ground to powder, are employed in flattening and polishing other hard substances, and its points, on account of their extreme hardness, are used in perforating and cutting other minerals ; yet its chief value in every age has consisted in its beauty and brilliancy as an ornament. And because it is the rarest, purest, and most beautiful gem of physical nature, every-where and always esteemed, possessing value seldom depreciated, and a brilliancy never dimmed, we have thought it proper to introduce it in this volume as the symbol of another jewel with which man is invested—one infinitely more valuable than any gathered from the mines of nature.

By modifying slightly a beautiful utterance of that gifted blind poetess of New York, Fanny Crosby, we have the following :

I know of a jewel whose luster
  Is purer and brighter than gold—
A jewel that sparkles forever,
  Whose value can never be told;
A jewel more precious than rubies,
  Or pearls from the depths of the sea—
A jewel, dear reader, worth keeping,
  A treasure for you and for me.

What a wonderful fact that each of us has been invested and charged with the keeping and culture of a jewel infinitely more durable than the diamond; possessing a thousand faculties of thought, will, and affection, of pleasure and pain, and of outshining forever its brightest luster as does the king of day the tiniest shell!

We obtain enlarged views, and often reach important and valuable conclusions, by comparison. The world never appears so small as when viewed in comparison with the heavenly bodies. The creature never becomes so insignificant as when placed in the scale with the Creator. Time never seems so short as when contrasted with eternity; and its moments seldom appear more valuable than when reckoned as sands of gold. It is therefore hoped that the youthful reader, at least, will gain some new and permanent impressions concerning his own importance and capabilities by a comparison of these gems of matter and of mind, and will be deterred from sacrificing the improvement of the latter for the possession of the former, as giddy thousands have done, discovering their sad mistake when there was left no place for repentance.

The human soul is a jewel of rare and transcendent mold. It is invested with the most exquisite faculties, and is susceptible of marvelous development. It has a swift perception of good and evil, a keen sense of honor and shame, of joy and woe, and is so poised in the scale of being that eternal destiny hinges upon its choice. But this jewel, like the diamond, has drifted away from its original relations, and lies buried in strange and calamitous associations amid the reefs and surges of ignorance and sin.

Probably but few of the diamonds that have drifted from their birthplaces have ever fallen into the hands of man. The chief search has always been along the earth's surface. Large, brilliant gems have probably collected between the reefs, and for ages have lain deeply covered in the bed of rivers, never to be exhumed. Others linger in neglected fields, and still others are trodden over by the ignorant or the savage, who never discover their real value. These wastes and losses are, however, unavoidable in the realms of physical nature.

This world, considered intellectually and morally, is a vast diamond field strewn in every part with richest gems. Some lie waiting, glistening upon the surface.   These are easily reached and soon gathered by the early toilers. Some are half buried, others quite concealed ; while far down, down, are strewn in wildest confusion and gloom myriads that can only be reached by immense digging, and polished by abundant friction.   Women with talent for the loftiest duties of their sphere crouch in rags amid the desolation of hovels, and weep under their sorrows and wrongs.   In native intellect they are piercing and discriminating, and could have ruled like Victoria.   With culture and opportunity they could have written like Harriet Beecher Stowe.   They have the emotions, the ambitions, and affections of a Florence Nightingale, but, alas ! they are buried in ignorance and neglect, and wasted with multiplied disappointments.   Ignorant women carry the hod in Vienna, draw the canal-boat, like beasts of burden, in Holland, and in a thousand other places in both hemispheres perform the most menial field service.   Given to physical labors only, they appear coarse and hardy to the last degree ; their arms are large and brawny, their voices coarse and harsh, while in countenance they exhibit little of the intellect, genius, or modesty of their sex. Their career is but little above the life of the beast. They are not disturbed with thoughts about choice apparel, beauty of complexion, or the exquisite proprieties of life. Thus they live and die in stupid squalor who with care and culture might have taught the sciences, polished the minds of their offspring, or graced a drawing-room.

Men are quarrying stone on Dix Island, digging coal in the mountains of Pennsylvania, and fishing in rowboats off Sandy Hook, who might have been professors in colleges, statesmen, admirals, and authors. Thousands live and die in penury—the day-servants of their equals—who might easily have risen to be masters of estates. Many wait supinely for fortune to overtake them who might have found it by diligence and thrift. Men and women of transcendent gifts fill our prisons, and bury themselves in confusion and shame through the perversion and abuse of their faculties.

There is a genuine nobility in all useful toil, which we would not be supposed to disparage. Some one must dig the coal, collect the ore, and scoop out the canal. Some one must clean the sewer, dust the carpet, sweep the chimney.

Some one must sprinkle the street, and black the boots. Some one must carry the hod, brush away the cobweb, scour the silver, and scrub in the kitchen. We cannot all forever wear white kids and appear on dress parade. The race would soon perish from the earth if all sought to be merchants, or bankers, or speculators, or tourists, or were given exclusively to literary pursuits. We need farms as much as cities, and factories as well as academies, and foundries are as useful as astronomical observatories. The world requires servants as well as proprietors, artisans as well as artists, laborers as well as men of letters.

And there is no disgrace in a worn garment, a bronzed countenance, a calloused hand, or muscles hardened with much toil. Manual toil is not only a providential necessity in the world, but an advantage and pleasure to every well-governed mind. No true gentleman was ever ashamed to dig in his garden, or to attend to the duties of any legitimate business. Indeed, the true gentleman never asks the most menial to perform what he is ashamed to do himself. A woman is none the less a lady, no less the accomplished queen of the circle, because she superintends in the laundry, gives examples in the kitchen, and "eats not the bread of idleness." The world will never allow the names and deeds of Peter the Great of Russia, of George Washington, of Elizabeth Fry, or Florence Nightingale to be forgotten. While favored with position, wealth, and culture, they nobly stooped—if stooping it may be called— to attend in person to the most laborious and trying duties of human life. They suffered no loss of dignity by familiarity with the navy yard, the camp, and the farm. They lost no beauty, no culture, no happiness, no honor, by visiting scenes of sadness in hospitals, in prisons, in dungeons or garrets.

But the great crime of the masses is in allowing their minds to habitually trail in the dust with their bodies. Created for high and ever-expanding contemplations, they feed their minds so persistently on the dust of their daily drudgery that they gather little else, and are never prepared for any but an inferior place among those of their own craft. Man is as indolent in mind and body; and because it is harder to study and think than to perform manual toil, vast multitudes tamely submit to be intellectually *buried diamonds*, who might easily rise to shine among the jewels of the world.

It is a virtue to toil patiently upon a farm, in a factory, a mine, or in a garret; to live in plainness and sobriety; and, when manifestly in the path of duty, and fully exerting one's best faculties, to be contented with our income and our surroundings. But it is a great crime to bury one's mind in willful ignorance, or one's moral power in corruption and sin. A blind or a hoodwinked man on the brow of a natural preci- pice will strain his eyes for light, and one buried alive will struggle to regain the surface. Yet unnumbered multitudes crowd the world who have never opened their eyes to the lofty possi- bilities of their being, and who refuse to be shocked by the disclosure of their appalling dangers. Intellectually, socially, and morally, they lie far below their proper level, empaneled in ignorance, poverty, and gloom, and, like the dead Lazarus in his rock-bound grave, make no effort to gain the rays of a higher sphere.

The intellect is as manifestly for development and employment as the muscles. Heaven and earth are filled with subjects of inquiry and contemplation. The Creator seeks to lift the thoughts of his creatures to his works and himself. His voice to them is: "Lift up your eyes on high, and behold who hath created these things, that bringeth out their host by number; he calleth them all by their names; by the greatness of his might, for that he is strong in power, not one faileth." "The heavens declare the glory of God, and the firmament showeth his handiwork." "The earth, also, is full of thy riches." What multitudes stroll about the world in quest of temporary pleasure or profit, but never entertain one lengthened inquiry about the blue heavens above them, the earth under their feet, the momentous facts of their own destiny, or their relationship to the Ruler of the universe! God pronounces a fearful "*woe*" on those that seek fleshly gratifications, but who "regard not the work of the Lord, neither consider the operations of his hands." Yet who will number the millions, even in enlightened countries, who have no intelligent theories concerning the revolutions of the earth, the action of the tides, the changes of the seasons, the nature and composition of the grosser elements; of the nature of light, heat, or of electricity; of the principles of optics or acoustics; of the properties of food, the true uses of medicines, or a thousand other things that fall within the range of their daily observations, and in which the operations of the Eternal are so wondrously manifested! They care as little about history as science, and, except their own brief experience, know nearly as little of time as of eternity. All these are, however, gifted by original endowment with mental abilities, and, if they would realize it, with abundant facilities for culture and usefulness. No toil, penury, or seclusion can lock up mind in an enlightened age and country. Voltaire studied in prison, Elihu Burritt at the anvil, and Thurlow Weed in early life wrapped his shoeless feet with rags, and over the drifted snow scoured the neighborhood for books, which he read by fire-light in the sugar-camp; Paul wrote his epistles in the prison at Rome; Bunyan penned his "Pilgrim's Progress" and six other books in the Bedford Jail; De Foe wrote his "Robinson Crusoe" and many political pamphlets in prison; Smollett wrote his "Sir Lancelot Greaves" while in close confinement; Grotius, early in the seventeenth century, prepared his "Annotation on the Gospels" while confined in the Castle of Loevenstein; Boethius wrote his "Consolations of Philosophy" while imprisoned at Pavia; Buchanan produced his "Paraphrase on the Psalms" while incarcerated in a Portuguese monastery; Cooper wrote his "Purgatory of Suicide" in the Stafford Jail; and Richard Baxter composed portions of his best works while detained in the King's Bench Prison. The Tower of London has been the theater of much literary toil and triumph. Within that dreary castle William Penn wrote his work "No Cross, no Crown;" Sir Walter Raleigh wrote his "History of the World;" Prior his "Alma; or, Progress of the Soul;" and Elliott his treatise on "The Monarchy of Man." Luther, shut up in the Wartburg, spent long days in translating the Scriptures; James Montgomery produced his first volume of poetry in the prison at York Castle; and Kossuth, the Hungarian patriot, mastered the English language during his two years' imprisonment at Buda.

These examples abundantly establish the fact that no seclusion, toil, poverty, misfortune, or combination of opposing forces, can effectually bar up the way of progress to an ambitious and

persevering mind.   Untoward circumstances
may temporarily delay the progress of a soul;
but gathering strength under defeats, it will
eventually burst through these difficulties as
did Samson the green withes which bound him.

The fields of the world are also as wide for
usefulness as for culture.   Every sphere, from
the hovel to the palace, affords scope for the
seed and the harvest.   The early Methodist
preachers of America sometimes addressed
weeping crowds through the grated windows
of their temporary prisons, and though continually persecuted and hampered with legal re-
strictions, they every-where gathered golden
sheaves for their Master's garner.   However
narrow may be the bounds of one's occupation,
the limits of his acquaintance, or the range of
his knowledge, he may still be useful.   Though
performing the most menial service in a mine,
a factory, or on a farm, he is brought in contact
with other minds whom he can influence and
mold.   Peter the Hermit, without learning or
eloquence, aroused all Europe with his tears
and earnest appeals.   The words of the invalid
confined for long years to his room find their
way into the street.   Languishing in the hos-

pital, or dying in a prison, one can impress on the minds of attendants and strangers lessons of wisdom that will never be forgotten. The conclusion is then easily reached, that if we want a field for culture, or "a field of labor, we can find it anywhere," whether blessed with poverty or riches, and in whatever portion of the earth the lines have to us fallen.

America is said at present to afford the best market in the world for diamonds. And is it not also true, that the widest scope is here afforded for intellectual and moral diamonds? What opportunities for men and women of thought and moral power! What facilities for polishing diamonds are also here afforded, such as no other nation can boast! And yet no fact is more patent than that the world every-where abounds with buried talent. Society groans continually under the burdens inflicted upon it by indolence and misdirected energy.

It will not do to conclude that the ignorant, groveling, vicious members of the community were formed for nothing better; that they prefer filth and drudgery and shame to cleanliness, respectability, independence, and honor; that they prefer a prison-cell to a cheerful home ; to starve on the scanty wages of crime rather than enjoy the rewards of honest toil ; that to them ignorance is indeed bliss, and that they have gained already the loftiest objects of their ambition.   It is not safe to conclude that if there is gold anywhere it will certainly burst forth and shine.   Many rich mines have been long concealed, and brought to light only by much digging.   Diamonds are often so buried in corruption that their value is quite unnoticed. "Some years ago a lady in the streets of Boston picked up from the side of the gutter what looked like an ordinary article of jewelry.   It was a brooch containing a large-sized stone in a rough setting of coarse gold.   At first she thought of throwing it away as an unclean thing of little value, but concluded to cleanse it and use it.   One evening the rays from a lamp falling full upon it made it glisten with brightest light, as of a star fallen from heaven.   The lady carried it to a lapidary, who assured her that the stone was a first-water brilliant of great value.   The rough setting was a freak of its original owner, and the finder had, by its coarseness, been deceived as to the superior worth of the precious jewel."

Does not this circumstance afford an instructive lesson as to the possible value of what some have regarded as merely the rubbish and waste of society? In examining objects we should do more than scan their exterior. The value of a diamond does not consist in the style of its setting. So also the value and strength of a mind cannot always be inferred from its occupation or habits, its society, or the texture of the garments that cover the body. Diamonds in the rough are scattered over all the fields of this world. They thickly stud the filthy sinks of our great cities; they are buried along all the marts of commerce; they are concealed in the tents that whiten the desert, the hovels that dot the plain, and in the flashing palaces that adorn the metropolis; they are buried in asylums, alms-houses, prisons, and infirmaries; they creep in the dust, and ride unnoticed, sometimes in carts and sometimes in carriages; they soar in mid-air, float on ships, and sound the deep in search of treasure.

In the ages past poverty and other depressing circumstances buried diamonds; now, they are buried amid opportunities and splendors. Then, they were concealed by seclusion and despotism, and because the ages afforded no light to reflect their brilliancy ; now, they are covered beneath the leaves of the tree of liberty, amid schools and churches, with the full-orbed glories of the latter day streaming around them. Young men of parts, whose golden opportuni- ties gave promise of a brilliant future, bury themselves in unworthy indulgences, spend a few years in revelry, and then their lamp goes out. Alas ! how many *brilliants* are hopelessly buried every year in gambling dens, drinking gardens, opera houses, and those unmentionable places of midnight resort. "Void of under- standing," they turn away from the glories of intellectual, virtuous day, to bury themselves in vicious shades. Enchanted by the siren song of present but forbidden and ruinous gratifications, they follow "straightway as an ox goeth to the slaughter, or as a fool to the correction of the stocks, until a dart strike through their liver; as a bird hasteth to the snare and knoweth not that it is for his life." Alas ! humanity is buried in other than the recognized cemeteries that dot the fair suburbs of our cities and towns. Society has its prisons, its dungeons, its buried work-houses, its vaulted chambers, with underground passage-ways, where myriads toil, and sport, and waste, and wait, and weep!

What was John Bunyan during the first twenty-five years of his life but a buried diamond? He was illiterate, profligate, dissolute. So shockingly profane that an abandoned woman, whose heart had long been a stranger to every sentiment of purity, on hearing his blasphemies exclaimed, " You are the most ungodly man for swearing I ever saw!" Who believed that selfish, gnarled, and morbid nature could be mellowed and changed into such depths of tenderness, made capable of such exact rectitude ; be made to blaze so surprisingly on earth, and stand up in history such a monument of moral purity? Who imagined that so much sublimity of conception, poetry of thought, and graphic purity of diction, could be evolved from that clouded, profane intellect? One would have been pronounced wild who had predicted that in coming generations a great literary light (Lord Macaulay) should style him "first of allegorists, as Demosthenes is first of orators, and Shakspeare first of dramatists," and rank Bunyan and Milton as

4

the only two *creative* minds of England during the latter half of the seventeenth century. Verily, a brilliant diamond was exhumed when, under the melting, transforming influence of the great Spirit, his soul awoke to righteousness and the conscious responsibility of its sublime existence.

What was John B. Gough during the first twenty-six years of his life but a buried jewel? True, there were faint glimmerings of the true gem manifested during his boyhood as he toiled on in cold neglect and poverty, sighing and praying for a brighter day. But at the age of nineteen the dark waters overwhelmed him, swept him onward, downward, gulfward, far below the strata of his proper humanity, where he lay for six years so deeply incrusted in the blackened filth of that region that scarcely any perceived that he was a precious gem. But at last the day for his unearthing dawned, since which the sparklings of his great soul have flashed joy and gladness into the hearts of thousands on two hemispheres.

CHAPTER III.

JEWELS IN DISGUISE.

MAN sadly intoxicated called at my door several years since and demanded a hearing. He was tall, stalwart, commanding in person, and somewhat graceful in manner. His clothes were filthy, his hat worn and slouched. He asked for food, which was cheerfully given. Next he begged for money, probably that he might continue his revel. He urged and urged, but was persistently refused. Turning to totter away, he cast back at me a wistful glance, and in a half-subdued tone exclaimed, "Don't think meanly of me, sir; I assure you I am a gentleman in disguise."

We will not affirm that all drunkards are well-bred gentlemen, or indeed gentlemen in any sense; yet some of them unquestionably once were, and all certainly possess qualities which might have been trained for honor and usefulness, and however sad their fall, ludicrous their appearance, or wretched their lives, we hazard nothing in asserting that they still, in an important sense, are *jewels in disguise.*

The plunge of the human soul into any of the voluptuous or sordid pleasures of sense is the most irrational and melancholy spectacle of time, and exceeded only by a still later plunge into a sea of eternal wretchedness, to which all streams of selfish pleasure inevitably tend, as rivers to the ocean ; and the loftier the altitude one has attained by sparkling gifts of nature, social position, intellectual or moral culture, the deeper and more frightful is the descent. A ball of gold descending from the altitude of a thousand feet will so bury itself in the hardest earth that all its glittering substance will be concealed ; but though covered, trodden under foot, and forgotten, it is still valuable ; and so with a fallen soul. Genius, learning, beauty, self-control, self-respect, indeed nearly every element of worth, may be so immured that it is passed by in cold neglect, despised, or forgotten—yet it is only a *buried jewel.*

The most forlorn, dejected, or even demented specimen in the whole family of man is but a masked jewel, a buried diamond, a concealed scintillation from the Eternal Orb of the universe. A diamond is a diamond whether glittering in the diadem of a prince or incrusted in crude earth and buried by a thousand feet of soil. Cover it with all the polluting substances of nature, it is still a gem. Gold may be ground to powder, thrown into fire or water, mixed with sand, but its intrinsic value is not destroyed. You may beat it until the plate is less than the three hundred and fifty thousandth part of an inch in thickness, yet it is the same precious metal, untarnished and unchanged in nature and value.

A fallen soul is tarnished by its voluntary alliance with evil, but it possesses numerous inherent and wondrous qualities of which it can never be divested. These original and essential endowments live when the soul has descended to deepest infamy. They are evinced in freaks of fiendish invention, in flashes of wit, of sarcasm, or of remorse ; in gleams of affection, of hope, or desire.

Man is a gem whether you find him in London, in Yeddo, in Kamtchatka, or in Terra del Fuego. Whether robed in the royalty of a

king, clad in the scanty habit of a serf, or quite
uncovered like the wild African ; whether lux-
uriating in a palace, shivering in a hovel, master in college of civilization, or servant in the
wilds of barbarism ; whether handling the treasures of an empire, digging in a damp mine, or
begging bread in the street ; whether shrewdly
grasping for the clue that lifts to fame's high
pinnacle, or feeling for the last black round in
the ladder of shame, his intrinsic importance
cannot be concealed.   It marks the melody in
the song of the saint, the revelry of the inebriate, the curses of the criminal, and the rav-
ings of the maniac.   In his deepest moral defection his whole nature still glows with anima-
tion and ambition.   Hence he appears great in
the midst of littleness, strong in weakness, wise
in the midst of folly, and lofty in the most
studied cruelty and meanness.   Brutalize him
as you may, you cannot make him a brute ;
enslave and beat him, you cannot make
him less than man ; rob, overpower, and crush
him, he will not be subdued.   His great
nature may be neglected, or so concealed or
debased by a sordid exterior as to challenge
more of derision than of respect, still the im-

portant fact remains unchanged—*he is a jewel in disguise.*

Nearly every individual has his own standard of excellence, by which he judges the qualities of others ; and not a few look with coldness or contempt on large classes of persons because their delinquencies or vices are simply unlike their own. The calculating miser abominates the voluptuary and the inebriate, who in turn despise him, while the gay lady of fashion looks with high contempt on them all. All are alike fallen, viewing every thing from a false stand-point, and through a clouded atmosphere.

Many people suppose the habitual drunkard to be so far fallen as to have utterly lost all ambition, pride, conscience, hope, and even desire itself, except to gratify the cravings of a morbid appetite. What cares that man for the memory of his wife who is found in a state of beastly intoxication at the hour appointed for her funeral ? Can any spark of manhood remain in him who sells for drink the loaf that should feed his starving child ? Can he be sensible of pride who daily disgraces the mother that bore him, the wife that loves him, and the children that bear his name ? Can any lofty aspirations lin-

ger where every step is a plunge into a still
deeper abyss of wretchedness and shame?
Can one be proud who is fallen so far? Can
real desire for better things dwell under those
maudlin, ghastly, melancholy features? To
these inquiries thousands are ready to answer
emphatically, No. And yet those who have
long wallowed in the deepest mire of dissipation have been recovered to tell us that the
inebriate is not always so complete a wreck as
is generally supposed. All the floods of alcohol
cannot drown his ambition, nor all its flames
consume his pride. It may stupefy at intervals,
but cannot long deaden the conscience or ob-
literate the memory. The remembrance of
sunny hours in the better days that have flown
away, the early lessons of wisdom and piety, the
multiplied ministries of kindness and love, are
at times brought to mind, filling the soul of the
most reckless with a poignant sorrow understood only by him who has endured it. Every
thing he meets suggests the melancholy contrast between the present and the past. The
landscape, the rill, the orchard, the garden, the
church spire, the tolling bell, the rollicking play
of the child, the countenance of the aged

woman, the sprightly trip of the little maid, and the strains of pleasant music, all are alike vocal, talking to him in saddest tones of his childhood, his early playground, his home of affection, of his mother, his sister, his school, his sanctuary in those days of innocence and joy before disgrace had mantled his brow. If these things could only be forgotten, and he become wholly a brute, his deplorable condition would be more tolerable ; but, alas ! the attributes of that great nature cannot be ignored or winked into silence. He may plunge and plunge, and seek concealment in all the cavernous depths of sin, yet in spite of himself he must still *remember* and *think* and *feel.* " He may fly for solace to the maddening bowl, and stun his enemy in the evening, but it will return to rend him like a giant in the morning." His fearful flight during intervals of awakening to the river, to the precipice, to stretch himself across the railroad track, invoking the pangs of a violent death to hide his disgrace, prove that he sees that he is a slave crouching under the sway of a remorseless tyrant, his better faculties quite concealed though not extinguished.

To some there comes in an instant, under

some apparently trivial circumstance, an awakening of pride of character, of self-respect, of hope, and a quickened resolution to reform. Gough gives numerous examples of this sudden resurrection of nobler sentiments among inebriates, occasioned, perhaps, by the song or the unstudied utterances of a child. He mentions the case of a miserable, despised man, pronounced by every body "a brute," who came to his home one day irritated with drink, and ready to vent his anger on all around him. His little boy, ten years old, came to the door, but seeing his intoxicated father attempted to escape. "Dick, come here! come here!" uttered in a stern, authoritative tone, brought him into his father's presence; but his little face was bloody, his lip cut, and his eye greatly swollen. "What have you been doing, Dick?" he inquired. The boy answered reluctantly, "I have been fighting, father." The man cared nothing about his boy's fighting, he was good at that himself; but he asked, "What have you been fighting about?" The boy replied, "Don't ask me, father, for I don't want to tell you." With a still fiercer tone he exclaimed, "Tell me what you have been fighting for!"

" I don't want to." Full of rage, he seized him by the collar and roared out, " Now tell me what you have been fighting about or I'll cut the life out of you ! " The poor boy plead piteously, but as he still hesitated to tell the cause of the juvenile duel he struck him a severe blow with his clenched fist, and thundered again, " Now tell me what you have been fighting for ! " Finding himself in the paws of a lion who cared not for his life, the poor child wiped away the bloody tear from his mangled eye, and hesitatingly sobbed out, " Well, father, there was a rude boy out there who told me my father was a poor old drunkard, and I whipped him, and if he ever tells me that again I'll whip him again." The turning-point in that man's dreadful career was reached. The affection of his boy, evinced in that bloody countenance and that sobbing utterance, stung his soul as with a thousand poisoned arrows. The concealed jewel was unmasked. He was saved. Years afterward, in relating the circumstance, he exclaimed, " O, Mr. Gough ! what could I say ? My boy, ten years of age, fighting for his father's reputation ! I tell you it had like to have killed me. How I loved that boy, my noble boy! I could have almost worshiped him."

Another drunken father, unable to obtain more drink, stole the Testament his little girl had received as a gift from her Sunday-school teacher and meanly bartered it for alcohol. Not long after she lay faint and gasping on a dying bed. Turning her wasted countenance toward her dissipated parent, she said, "Father, when I go to heaven, suppose Jesus should ask me what you did with my little Testament, what shall I tell him?" That artless question, like a flash of lightning, pierced him through and through, and before she died he held her little hands in his, crying, "God be merciful to me a sinner!"

Turning from the drunkard to the miser, we encounter an entirely different character. The one is a creature of appetite, the other of passion. One in his frenzy squanders every thing, the other deliberately retains and hoards all. A miser is one who lives for earthly accumulations, usually converting all his treasures into gold or silver, which he silently secretes, clings to it until death, and ardently loves it for its own sake. Possessed of vast wealth, he wears the garb of the beggar, lives in a lonely garret, is nipped with frosts, scorched with heat, and pinched with hunger and disease. Late at night, when others are asleep, he bends with marvelous interest over his shining treasure. The pickpocket and burglar have never thought of searching for his possessions ; some have even pitied his poverty, while by the many he has been unnoticed and unknown. Finally he dies, and lo, in an iron-bound chest in some secret hiding-place are found thousands of dollars, much of the coin having, perhaps, been in his possession for half a life-time. Acquisitiveness with him became a consuming passion, swallowing up all thoughts of benevolence, all love of display, and even the desire for the ordinary comforts of life. Many are covetous, though but few are capable of being misers. Most people seek money as the means to something else, but with the miser it is the end of all coveted good. Some years since a well-known Parisian banker (Mr. Ostervald) died in his native city literally of want. So intent was this man on retaining his money, that within a few days of his death no importunities could induce him to purchase a piece of meat for the purpose of making him a soup. "'Tis true," said he, "I should not dislike the soup, but I have no appetite for the meat ; what, then, is to become of that ?" While thus dying of self-imposed starvation, lest he should be compelled to lose or give away a piece of meat, there was tied around his neck a silken bag which contained eight hundred bank-notes of a thousand francs each, or an amount about equal to one hundred and fifty thousand dollars. Mr. Wesley mentions the case of a man who, with an income of two hundred pounds a year, purchased each week a penny's worth of parsnips at the market, which he boiled in a large quantity of water. By drinking the water and eating the parsnips he entirely subsisted for a long period on a penny a week.

While writing this volume we clipped from a daily paper the following : "Died, in San Francisco, April 13, 1872, Dr. William Hewer, an English miser, long a noted character in San Francisco. He was found dead on a pile of rags in his room, which had not been swept in fourteen years. Over sixty thousand dollars in gold were found in this apartment." Robert Pollok, with his usual point and strength, has

given us a striking description of the miser.
He says:

"But there was one in folly farther gone;
With eye awry, incurable and wild,
The laughing-stock of devils, and of men,
And by his guardian angel quite giv'n up—
The miser, who with dust inanimate
Held wedded intercourse. Ill-guided wretch!
Thou mightest have seen him at the midnight hour
When good men slept, and in light-wingéd dreams
Ascended up to God—in wasteful hall,
With vigilance and fasting worn to skin
And bone, and wrapped in most debasing rags—
Thou mightest have seen him bending o'er his heaps,
And holding strange communion with his gold;
And, as his thievish fancy seemed to hear
The night-man's foot approach, starting alarmed,
And in his old, decrepit, withered hand,
That palsy shook, grasping the yellow earth
To make it sure. Of all God made upright,
And in their nostrils breathed a living soul,
Most fallen, most prone, most earthly, most debased;
Of all that sold eternity for time,
None bargained on so easy terms with death.
Illustrious fool! Nay, most inhuman wretch!
He sat among his bags, and with a look
Which hell might be ashamed of, drove the poor
Away unalmsed; and midst abundance died:
Sorest of evils! died of utter want."

The soul of even the miser is nevertheless a
disguised jewel. Its faculties are sadly perverted, but might have been turned to good
account. A story is told of a young man who

picked up a sovereign some one had lost in the road. Greatly elated with his success, he ever afterward as he walked kept his eye steadfastly on the ground in hopes of finding more, and during his long life he did pick up considerable gold and silver. But through all this period he looked so perpetually downward that he saw not the verdure of the smiling fields, nor the brightness of the heavens above him, and when he died, a rich old man, he knew this fair earth only as a dirty road on which to pick up money. This man had powers capable of higher pursuits, but they were debased, and never made to answer the true end of their creation.

The perfect miser is probably the most hopeless character in the world. The drunkard, the burglar, the voluptuary, and the gambler mingle in some society, retain the traces of some virtues, and evince some fluctuations of feeling, hence there are avenues through which they may be reached. But the miser seeks solitude, ignores every thing but his plans of gain, linking himself only to his molten god. By resisting conscience, and crushing every sympathetic impulse, his nature becomes obdurate and impenetrable, like the fire-hardened clay, impervious alike to light or heat.

What miserable object is that stumbling over the curbstone to escape the ponderous cart-wheel? Now that form grazes the lamp-post, reels against the door of a dingy shop, and falls prostrate on the slippery pavement. Let us draw near. Ah! now I see; it is the miserable wreck of a woman—and O, what a wreck! Covered with dirt, her tattered garments but half conceal her person. Her head is bare, save the long black ornament nature provided, which evinces great want of care. Her feet are nearly naked, her hands, arms, and neck deeply discolored. She has seen but thirty summers, but her staggering gait, her bronzed complexion, her battered face, her expressionless eye, show ravages worse than those of years.

But she has not been always thus. She was born in a pleasant cottage, surrounded with wealth and luxury. Her father went on 'Change, handled rich wares, owned ships, and carried stocks. When he had an hour of leisure he hastened home, saluted his wife, looked into the blue eyes of his smiling child,

5

petted and kissed her, and called her his little
queen. Servants rocked her, drove away the
fly, carried her in their arms, and wealthy
neighbors admired her. The heart of her
fond mother glowed with silent pride over the
brightening luster of her little gem. Those
were days of innocent joy, little understood by
her, and destined soon to fly away never to
return. This period was the deep calm preceding the storm which burst upon her life-
voyage, darkening her sky, sweeping away her
protectors, lashing and discoloring her nature,
until she lies as you see, a stranded wreck, with
scarcely the vestige of a *woman* or of humanity
recognizable. A train of reverses overwhelmed
her father. Her frail mother died of disappointment, leaving her child at a tender age
without means or protection. The beauty of
her gifted nature made her a brilliant mark for
the destroyer and accelerated her ruin. Kind
words, much longed-for, came in the voice of
the deceiver, but they were followed by deser-
tion, scorn, and the gall of the outcast. She
had no father to defend her, no mother to pity
or weep over her misfortune. No friendly
retreat opened its door. No heart bled over

her woe, and no arms of generous help came to her relief. One false step led to another, and the descent became increasingly rapid and frightful, until she became the dreadful spectacle before you, her haggard form disclosing the ravages of wasting vices. But is she not a thousand times more to be pitied than despised ? Is she not too bright and valuable a jewel, though vailed in this dreadful garb, to be forever lost ? Her nature has become exceedingly stolid. You cannot move her with contempt, or ridicule, or scorn, or blows, or threats. She has borne all these until her soul, as her body, has become callous. But do not count her a brute. Her nature still answers to Dickens' description of Mrs. Todgers, who, he says, "was a hard woman, yet in her heart, away up a great many stairs, there was a door, and on that door was written—*Woman.*" In the depths of her discolored nature still linger the traces of the modest, affectionate, confiding girl. She has not lost all horror of sin, nor all desire for goodness. A hundred times she has wept over her crimes, and attempted reformation. More than once in the gray twilight of the morning she has laid her throbbing temples on her mother's grave, and with scalding tears has vowed again to be good, though this was followed by another plunge to a deeper degradation. There remains still one door of approach to the temple of her better nature. This door is bolted and guarded, yet it will yield to the pressure of unselfish *Christian tenderness.* Under the melody of hallowed song, the burning appeals of a loving heart, or the subduing power of prevailing prayer, the tide of pent-up emotion will burst forth accompanied by the blush of animated hope, the quailing eye, the softened tone of confession, penitence, and supplication. She is simply a *jewel in disguise,* and God's earnest miners are every day gathering diamonds from the gutters and sewers of earth's slimy fields that shall glitter forever in the sparkling diadem of the world's Redeemer.

What is a gay young woman of wealth, pleasure, and fashion, but a jewel in disguise? She has been divinely invested with sterling capacity, and might teach, relieve, and save ; but she is buried soul and body under the plumes of fashion, and lives and dies as uselessly as the butterfly. How can those delicate feet run on errands of mercy for the relief of the helpless and sorrowful? They are weary already with shopping and waltzing. How can those snow-white hands steady the tottering, or carry the burden of her who is ready to perish? They have not seen the sun for a year, and the blue veins disclose the fact that they are dying for want of healthy activity. This poor creature is perpetually wearied with the hollow aimlessness of her existence, trailing about in long and tightly-fitted garments, covered with flounces, fringes, and laces. The lassitude resulting from evening rides, theaters, and late parties has taken away all desire for usefulness, if any ever existed. Perhaps she attends a fashionable church occasionally on pleasant Sabbath mornings, but how can she attain to thoughts of a Change of Heart, of Providence, of the Resurrection, or Eternity? How be interested in matters of Sunday-schools or Missions when such an array of choice bonnets, basques, shawls, and gorgeous trimmings are floating around her? How can she instruct orphan children, or spend time to relieve or counsel a friendless woman as long as those questions with the French dressmaker remain unsettled—whether the new silk overskirt shall be in the Jessamine, Juliet, Adrienne, the Mordaunt, Zerlina, or Casilda style ; whether the rich velvet basque shall be of the Imogen, Evalie, or Mignon ; and whether loose, gored, or double-breasted ?   Ought she not to have a new Lulu jacket, and a Talma of the latest style ? A new tight-fitting polonaise could be worn occasionally if very richly trimmed.   What of the Dean, Felina, or Dolly Varden styles ?   At how many of the watering-places shall she go to spend portions of the heated term ? and what shall be the nature and variety of her outfit ? What shall be the programme for entertainments, receptions, and parties during the autumn and winter ?   These and similar thoughts occupy all her mind.   She has not a moment for prayer or usefulness, or a thought for humanity or eternity.   The annual cost of her wardrobe would purchase a plantation.   In her visit to Saratoga she carries more changes of raiment, and as many jewels and valuables, as did the Queen of Sheba in her visit to Solomon. Her notions of life are all inflated.   Life is a bubble and a dream, and after a brief and gay career, her remains, in costly vestments, followed by a long and brilliant procession, find their place beneath the adornments of the cemetery! But she was buried while she lived, walled in by selfishness and pride, by notions of caste, and by excessive love of ease, of gayety, and pleasure.

Wealthy parents bury their children, particularly their daughters, amid luxuries and the conventionalities of fashionable society. Many young women among the rich have sterling ambitions, real energy, and force of character, but these are dwarfed because perpetually restrained and bound down by the false demands of fashion. A young man in the same circle grows restive, breaks the shackles, and plunges into business amid the hearty applause of the community. But let the daughter inquire for something to tax her faculties, and she is pointed to her piano, to her croquet-ground, to her French dressmaker, and advised to abandon all schemes of importance save hunting for a rich husband. We shall never know how many young ladies, capable of being genuine heroines, real diamonds, are buried or disguised under the immense fortunes of successful merchants, bankers, and proprietors of real estate.

As the ancient heathen sacrificed their children
to their molten gods, so do these at the shrine
of fashion and mammon.   Every thing most
worthy, important, and eternal is sacrificed to
the trivial and the ephemeral.   As in the dream
of Pharaoh, the lean kine devour the fat kine.
Love of display, of ease, and of self consumes
all thoughts of being serviceable to man, and
reverent or obedient to God.   Heaven is swal-
lowed by earth, and eternity by time.

Reader, what is your real *status* in the realm
of intellect, and in the world of morals and religion ?   What powers of your mind and of
your heart have the predominance ?   Have you
sought by suitable reading, meditation, and
prayer ; by humility, self-denial, and useful toil,
to assiduously cultivate your better faculties ?
Is it your daily and absorbing study to know
how to be true, useful, intelligent, and wise ; to
know how to so direct and develop your powers as to most improve humanity and honor
God ?   If to these inquiries an affirmative response is given, though your progress has hitherto appeared slow, and your success moderate,
you have reason to be encouraged.   The intellectual and moral graces of your soul will yet

burst forth with a glow, with a fervor and a luster of which you have at present no adequate conception. But if the love of ease, or of display, or of wealth ; the gratification of appetite, or the pursuit of empty honors, has ruled your heart and your life, then, with all your endowments and progress, you still are, and may forever remain, only—*a jewel in disguise.*

CHAPTER IV.

POLISHING ROUGH DIAMONDS.

HE processes by which a diamond is prepared for use are exceedingly slow and painful, and as all diamonds are found in the rough, a handsomely cut stone is all the more valuable in consequence of the expense attending its polishing. The surface form of the diamond is changed by taking advantage of its cleavage by abrasion with its own powder, and by friction with another diamond. All flaws are removed if possible by the skillful lapidary by cleaving it, otherwise it must be sawed with an iron wire covered with diamond powder, which is a tedious process, as the wire is usually worn in two when drawn five or six times across the jewel. After the portions containing flaws have been removed the stone is fixed to the end of a stick in strong cement, leaving the part projecting which is to be cut, and another diamond is fixed in a similar manner, and the two rubbed together until facets are produced. By changing the position other and still other facets are produced, until the desired form is obtained. A revolving wheel of soft iron, covered with diamond powder, is used in completing the polish. Sometimes an experienced workman will consume many days in producing a single facet, at other times one is produced in a few hours. The cutting of large and valuable diamonds is a very critical undertaking, as a workman may in a moment destroy more than he can earn in a life-time.

The immortal diamond, of which these sparkling gems of nature are but the figure, comes into being also in an unpolished condition, and requires no small amount of abrasion to fit it for the exalted uses contemplated by the Creator in its formation. The larger part by far of those who have attained to special distinction in the world were in their early beginnings quite unpromising, and considered by the most hopeful, at the very best, as only *diamonds in the rough*. The uprisings of these intellectual gems from profoundest obscurity to astonish the world with inventions, charm with marvelous genius, dazzle with learning or eloquence, or to lead its gifted minds by the depths of their wisdom, have been in all times matters of more than transient interest. As when a large, rich diamond has been unexpectedly discovered the valleys of a neglected district are speedily brought into importance, so extraordinary exhibitions of talent or genius suddenly clothe one's earlier career, though hitherto quite unnoticed, with magical interest. Curious critics are at once ready to embark on a voyage of discovery in quest of one's genealogy, the cot of his birth, the school, associations, habits, books, and whatever else are supposed to have entered into his formation. Theories are invented, matters of trivial importance strangely magnified, and manufactured vagaries trumpeted around the world. Fierce word-battles have been fought about the birthplace of Homer and the facts of his existence. The shades of Attica have been pierced to find the lamp and pebbles of Demosthenes. Ingenious minds have tracked the father of John Milton through the royal forests of Oxfordshire, described the cradle in which Goldsmith was rocked at Kilkenny, and traced the history of Irving's an-

cestors for several centuries in the Orkney
Isles back to the armor-bearer of the illustrious
Bruce.

The hereditary gentry of the world have
presumed to ask what right a Brotherton, a
mere factory boy, has to a seat in Parliament?
a Newton, the son of an indigent yeoman, to
grasp the noblest laurels in philosophy? a
Nelson, the son of an obscure clergyman, to
become ruler of the seas? a Luther, the offspring of an industrious ore-digger, to become
one of the world's chief ministers? or a Lincoln,
a frontier farm-laborer, to the presidential chair
in an enlightened nation? The common sense
of the ages has, however, accorded the palm
to him whose capacity and toil have nobly won
it, irrespective of previous relationship, whether
to master or minion.

A surprising proportion of illustrious men,
whose names now grace as with gilded characters the pages of history, not only sprang from
obscure families and were bred in penury, but
exhibited in their early years a dullness almost
crushing the hopes of their parents and dis-
couraging their teachers and themselves. Some
appeared alike destitute of penetration and

memory, and of a desire to either know or do. Unlike West, who declared that his mother's encouraging kiss made him a painter, some of these remained for years perfectly imperturbable amid the flatteries and threats of friend and foe. Whenever their talent was brought into healthy competition they suddenly paled in the luster of others, and shrank into obscurity; and when experiment or favoritism placed them at the head of the class, they preserved their identity by as speedily gravitating to the *inevitable bottom.*

When Isaac Newton, afterward Sir Isaac, was at school in Skillington, he stood for a long period at the foot of one of the lowest classes, and was such an unmitigated dunce that many despaired of his ever knowing any thing. Isaac Barrows, the distinguished mathematician and divine, when at school at the Charter House was remarkable for his idleness, insolence, and pugnacious habits. He appeared to have been formed for an ignorant, imbruted pugilist. His stupidity and obstinacy were a perpetual grief to his parents, and his father was once heard to say that if it pleased God to remove any of his children he hoped it would be Isaac, the least promising of them all. Jonathan Swift, afterward the brilliant Dean of St. Patrick's, was a most indifferent and reckless student, squandering time, and so unmindful of authority as to incur seventy penalties and censures in two years, and after suffering many insults was further disgraced by receiving his bachelor's degree after the proper time, and *Speciali gratia.* Adam Clarke, the learned Wesleyan commentator, ranked among the dullest of boys until he passed his eighth year. Thomas Chalmers, and a youth of similar age, who afterward became Professor of Moral Philosophy at St. Andrews, were so stupid and unmanageable that the disheartened teacher of the parish school expelled them both as quite unworthy of further effort. Walter Scott, at a later period Sir Walter, while at school was an expert at a "bicker," but lame and tame at a lesson. Professor Dalzell, at the Edinburgh University, pronounced upon him the unfounded sentence and prediction, " Dunce you are, and dunce you will remain." Sheridan's mother, grieved by his unyielding stolidity, presented him to a new tutor with this uncomplimentary statement, " He is an incorrigible dunce." Oliver Goldsmith was sadly lacking in good sense through, at least, the first half of his career, and after his death was described by his early teacher as a boy "*impenetrably dull.*" Alfieri, the Italian Count and terse dramatic poet, spent eight years in academic shades without attaining the rudiments of an education ; and John Howard spent seven years in school to very little purpose. Robert Clyde, who died Lord Baron of Plassey, and the far-famed conqueror of India, was in youth so adverse to study, and so violent and treacherous in temper, that his father, fearful of his future, shipped him to Madras as a subordinate *attaché* of the East India Company. Hugh Miller, at the Grammar School at Cromarty, stood "usually at the nether end of a very poor class." No one discovered any thing remarkable in the early career of Wellington, Napoleon, Franklin, Sir Humphrey Davy, Watts, Burns, Washington, Elihu Burritt, Edward Hitchcock, and many more who have since become distinguished.

Perhaps the youthful reader is quite impatient to know how the buried jewel in their nature was reached ; how their groveling thoughts were, like the rocket, suddenly made to flash upward, and by what mysterious abrasions they attained the luster that filled their elevated sphere of greatness. Man is not, like the diamond, absolutely passive. He is divinely favored with the power of unearthing himself— of feeling his way into the higher realms of existence, and to the exercise of this inherent power must we look for the brilliant changes in men's intellectual career more than to all other sources combined. By some circumstance a dull boy becomes suddenly conscious that he possesses latent and hitherto unemployed powers. This appears to have flashed through the minds of some while burning under a sense of shame ; of others, by the dawnings of lofty ambitions ; and of still others, under the smart of provocations.

After Newton had stood at the foot of his class until all supposed him a fixture, the boy next above him, in a freak of petulance, and supposing him perfectly stolid, administered to him a smart kick. That fortunate kick broke the shell of his slumbering genius, and gathering energy he forthwith challenged his assailant to a youthful duel, and dealt him a much-deserved

drubbing. Having vanquished his antagonist
in the yard, he resolved to repeat it in the
school, and soon rose not only to the head of
the class, but of the school as well. And it
was by the force of the same will, and of similar
persistent and unflagging application, that he
continued to rise ever afterward until the world
was glad to enshrine his name in the temple of
fame. Adam Clarke was similarly aroused by
the sarcasm of a school-fellow, after which he
made rapid progress in every thing except
mathematics. Curran, the Irish orator, when
at school was familiarly known as " Stuttering
Jack," which led to numerous and deep embarrassments. At a debating club he arose to
speak, but finding himself speechless he sat
down in confusion. A witty antagonist re-
ferred to him as " *Orator Mum*," bringing down
the house with roars of laughter. Curran's
Irish combatables now came to the rescue, and
he replied in a triumphant speech, his first
exhibition of real oratory. This consciousness
of ability, this self-respect, form an indispensa-
ble foundation for large development, leading
to important undertakings and surprising results. Newton believed he could improve the

telescopes of his day; hence he pursued his investigations until led to exchange the refracting lens for the reflecting. Herschel believed he could perfect his seven-foot reflector, though untaught; and though he failed in adjusting the specula one hundred and ninety-nine times, he persevered, and the two hundredth experiment proved successful.

All truly great and successful men perceive, and have also shown, that the period of development extends through one's entire career; hence, like the persevering lapidary, they have steadily held the diamond to the wheel from year to year, conscious that ultimate triumph must crown their exertions. Though pronounced dunces, perhaps, at the beginning, they were not of the life-long kind, counting every thing valuable too high for their reach or too deep for their soundings. When clearly mistaken or in the wrong they have hastily changed front. When they awoke to the fact that their education had been neglected, they immediately undertook the remedy with intensest application, not faltering because schooldays were ended. School training is valuable chiefly from the contact with advanced minds

and the habit formed of systematic and protracted application. But no amount of mere
academic training ever made one illustrious,
and none but a veritable self-made dunce
ever sat down in indolent despair because he
had not enjoyed it. Men in every sphere become educated and great by *toil and thought.*
Putting ideas into one's head is not educating,
any more than putting wheat into the mill is
grinding. Thoughts forced into the mind by
teachers, unless inwardly studied, are as worthless as bread injected into the stomach of the
dead. All great men have taught their powers
the art of perpetual work, and when this is
once accomplished one will secure education
anywhere and under almost any circumstances.
Multitudes of illustrious men would have died
in obscurity had they not practiced on the
principle presented in the reply of Edward
Stone to the Duke of Argyle, who inquired
how he, a gardener's boy, had learned to read
Latin. He replied, " One needs only to know
the English alphabet to learn every thing else
he wishes." Dr. Dempster, late President of
the Garrett Biblical Institute, was self-taught
in the Methodist itinerancy. He mastered, like

Adam Clarke, one dead language after another, in privacy, and rose to be a master among scholars. Eliphalet Nott, D.D., for fifty-six years President of Union College, was also self-educated. He pursued his studies alone, toiling on the farm, entering Brown University just six weeks previous to the close of the term, and was graduated with the class. Alfieri at the age of twenty-seven went back to grammar, and studied the rudiments of learning which he had neglected at school. He spent years in middle life in the mountains of Piedmont with books and an occasional literary companion, and at forty-six took up the study of Greek. Dr. Edward Hitchcock enjoyed only the most limited facilities of early schooling, but by incessant private application rose to the first rank of American scholarship, publishing over twenty volumes, some of which have been deservedly popular in two hemispheres. Washington Irving, also, never attended either college or academy; Goldsmith formed no attachment for literature until he was thirty; Arkwright began the study of grammar at fifty; Sir Henry Spelman, the English antiquarian, began science at fifty-five; Benjamin Franklin at twenty-seven took up the study of the Latin, Italian, French, and Spanish languages, and did not begin in earnest with natural philosophy until he was nearly fifty. While crossing the Atlantic on his Government mission to France, in 1776, and at the age of seventy years, he studied out the theory of the Gulf Stream, and was the first to explain that interesting problem.

Most of these brilliant lights, known to us chiefly by their literary productions, were also through life involved in the incessant prosecution of other pursuits. They never waited for leisure, or brooked the idea of abandoning study under the pressure of business. They were miserly of time, turning its smallest fractions to the best account. Ben Jonson is said to have toiled at the building of Lincoln's Inn with "a trowel in his hand and a book in his pocket." Hugh Miller studied geology while toiling in the quarries of Cromarty; and Elihu Burritt mastered over twenty languages before be abandoned his trade at the anvil, since which he has added as many more to the list, while involved in other active pursuits. Clive developed himself amid the savages of the East Indies ; Bloomfield composed his best poem on a shoemaker's bench, in a garret ; and Herschel, in deepest poverty, studied astronomy at Bath, playing an organ for his board.   Dr. Darwin, the English physiologist and poet, composed several books while riding among his patients ; Charles Wesley thought out his best hymns on horseback ; Kirke White learned Greek while walking to and from a lawyer's office ; and Albert Barnes wrote all his books before nine in the morning, amid the labors of a busy pastorate.   Dickens wrote most of his books while filling the chair of an editor.   Milton was a teacher and a busy State officer, and wrote more political treatises than we are now willing to read.   Lord Bacon was, through much of his life, an industrious lawyer, and advanced from this to important State appointments.   Shakspeare was an actor, and the manager of his own theater, writing all his plays for his own use, and with no apparent ambition for literary fame.   Greeley, Bryant, Stevens, and Holland have brought out their best works in the snatches of time redeemed from their laborious undertakings as editors of influential journals.   Baxter, Calvin, Farel, Cranmer, Hooper, Hooker, Boston, Wesley, Fletcher, Watson, Brownlee, and Edwards were ministers, so abundant in pulpit and pastoral labors, so involved in controversies, missionary enterprises, and other labors, that we wonder where they found time for deep literary pursuits. Their examples prove, however, that an active business career does not prevent the highest scientific attainments, or the most extensive and gifted authorship, by those who know the value of time and are intent on its improvement. The real secret of success is this : some become wealthy, learned, and great by simply turning to account what others throw away.

The career of earth's brightest intellects has been also marked by an *unbending purpose* to *excel.* Discouragements crowd the path of all, though not in an equal degree, requiring frequently the tact of an Alexander to cut the Gordian knot. Opulent advantages are of small value unless promptly improved, and ordinary embarrassments, to a sterling mind, are only calculated to make success the more triumphant. No one ever rose above his ambitions, or attained to any eminence without first resolving to pay the price and remain deaf to every other solicitation. And however crowded may be the ordinary walks of life, there is always scope for more laborers in the elevated spheres of human action. When Daniel Webster was told that the field of law was overrun with barristers, and that he should not think of turning his attention to such a crowded arena, he significantly replied, " There is room enough at the top," and evidently resolved to find the open space. Few men have ever attained to great eminence without such gigantic struggles as the many are unwilling to put forth. As they rise to higher planes of thought they encounter prejudice and sometimes envy. The most illustrious minds have at certain periods in their career appeared to the masses of their contemporaries like sublime simpletons, fitly illustrating Solomon's declaration, " Though thou shouldst bray a fool in a mortar with a pestle, yet will not his folly depart from him." The early career of Disraeli, the English Premier, both as author and orator, affords a striking example. He was certainly "brayed" in every thing but a " mortar," and with every thing but a " pestle," yet he held bravely on, saying, when utterly laughed down in Parliament, " I will sit down now, but the time will

come when you will hear me ;" which prophecy
was long since fulfilled.

Advanced minds are often misunderstood,
and their labors disparaged, if not attributed
to the worst motives. Socrates was charged
with corrupting the youth of his time because
his thoughts towered above the idolatries of the
age, and he was accordingly put to death.   All
Ephesus went off in a transport of rage because Paul could not glorify Diana.   Galileo
suffered deep persecution through life, and was
denied ordinary burial after death, because his
philosophical discoveries were in advance of his
contemporaries. Harvey lost nearly all his practice as a physician by publishing his discovery
of the circulation of the blood, and was stigma-
tized as a "fool" by the medical fraternity.
Kepler, Newton, Roger Bacon, and Locke were
pronounced heretics, infidels, or gross material-
ists.   All the reformers, as well as the Wesleys,
Whitefield, and Edwards, suffered violent opposition and obloquy.   They were branded as
hypocrites, false teachers, and usurpers, chiefly
because they lived in higher realms of thought,
attained to a deeper experience, and were
moved by purer impulses than those around

them. Their triumph resulted from their hearty adoption of the apostles' motto : " None of these things move me, neither count I my life dear unto myself, so that I might finish my course with joy, and the ministry I have received of the Lord Jesus."

Most of those distinguished men who flourished in the seventeenth and eighteenth centuries pursued their researches and toils solely from a love of truth and of souls. Calvin is said to have reaped no pecuniary reward from his vigorous pen. Milton sold his immortal " Paradise Lost" for five pounds, and Bunyan received but a trifle from his " Pilgrim's Progress." The copyright on Newton's *Principia* brought its gifted author but inconsiderable returns, which was true of nearly all the solid works of that period. Hume's early publications fell dead from the press, though he afterward attained popularity and fortune. Irving's renowned " Sketch Book," backed by the influence of Walter Scott, was rejected by the English publishers, after which the defeated but persistent author issued it on his own account. The proportion of those early authors who secured wealth from their toils to those who were poorly paid, or not at all, is as the proportion of those giant trees of California to the millions in the American forests. Yet they shrank from no sacrifice or toil; no amount of pains was spared for the best accomplishment of a great work. Literary men, above all others, are lavish in the bestowment of time, toil, and money on their undertakings, though they have the most uncertain prospects of reward.

Adam Clarke toiled forty-eight years over his Commentary; Webster devoted thirty of the best years of his life to his Dictionary, which in its present form has cost fully one hundred years of incessant literary application; Whedon studied twenty-five years on his great work on the Will; Watt studied thirty years on his condensing engine; and Ericsson twenty years on his floating battery, the Monitor. The record of the great is not the freak of fortune, but is inscribed in lines of effort and devotion, sustained by a purpose and fed by an enthusiasm so ardent as to consume fortune, favor, and often life itself.

Samuel Smiles, in his work on " Character," has truly said, " The work of some of the greatest discoverers has been done in the midst of

persecutions, difficulty, and suffering. Columbus, who discovered the New World, and gave
it as a heritage to the Old, was in his life-time
persecuted, maligned, and plundered by those
whom he had enriched. Mungo Park's drown-
ing agony in the African river, which he had
discovered, but which he was not to live to
describe ; Clapperton's perishing of fever on
the banks of the great lake, in the heart of the
same continent, which was afterward to be re-
discovered and described by other explorers ;
Franklin's perishing in the snow—it might be
after he had solved the long-sought problem of
the North-west passage—are among the most
melancholy events in the history of enterprise
and genius."

Persons of transcendent genius or of extraordinary discoveries well know that they must
and can afford to wait for the appreciation of
the world. Sir Isaac Newton triumphantly
overturned the philosophical system of Des
Cartes ; yet so violent was the opposition to
his views on the Continent that at his death it
was estimated he had not over twenty followers
outside of England, though his *Principia* had
been forty years before the world. Time

usually clears away obscurities, placing ultimately one's record in its true light ; but if this
fails, eternity will disclose all, so that the good
and the evil will find their appropriate rewards.

We ought to encourage young people of both
sexes, whose education has from any cause been
neglected, who have sighed for better opportunities, or whose minds have been of slow and imperfect development. Nearly every community
has a class of clumsy, awkward, ungainly boys,
and of girls not particularly prized for their
brilliant intuitions. These are often ridiculed
by their associates, and neglected by their
teachers and friends. If the eye of such a
youth runs over these pages, let him take cour-
age. Some minds do not open for the rapid
mastery of study until comparatively late in life.
Some memories grasp every thing as soon as
presented to-day, and have lost it all by to-
morrow ; while others are slow and unskillful
in the reception of facts, but retain forever all
they grasp. Remember that your whole career,
both in time and eternity, is for improvement ;
and we have shown how, in a multitude of instances, the dunces have by application become
illustrious. Education is not of transient value.

An inquiring, well-poised mind turns all its reading, observation, and experience to some valuable account, and these habits of close observation, of intense and useful application of talents and time, give, after all, the only zest to life. How gloomy is a prison to a stupid profligate who has no ambition to be a student! The hours lie upon his mind as bags of sand. All is gloom, because no intellectual lamp sheds its radiance through his soul ; but the student turns his cell into a study and a laboratory. Many great and good men, and women too, have dwelt in prison since John the Baptist was beheaded in his cell. They have wept, and prayed, and counseled, and planned, and fought, and triumphed there. The world would be poor to-day without the books written in prison. The nations have often experienced good because the sighings of the thoughtful prisoner have entered the ear of the Lord of Sabaoth.

Without these habits of application travel is a weariness and a discomfort. Crossing the Alps, the Great Desert, or the Rocky Mountains to the indolent, thoughtless man is a tedious exposure. His mind is occupied with the creaking of the diligence, the drifting of the sand, or the rumbling of the cars, and he comes to the end of his journey dusty, drowsy, petulant, and disgusted. Another has found it an exquisite pleasure—one unbroken revel amid the original and undisturbed beauties of nature. He has classified the plants, collected the testimony of the rocks, studied the nature and habits of the animals, and been charmed with the variety and plumage of the feathered tribes. He has named and numbered the mountains, ascertained their height, direction, and formation. The beetling cliff poised in mid-air is not to his eye in vain, nor the placid lake smiling in unbroken solitudes, nor the channels of the rivers cut in graceful curves, nor the wild cascade, with its shelving sides and dashing waters. Proportion and form and magnitude find place in his mind, as well as utility and beauty. To his mind it is not in vain that there are colorings in the crystal and in the foliage, blended hues in the rainbow, golden glories in the sunset, and gems in the mine. A thousand beauties start into existence every-where to attract his eye, and his ears are greeted with the symphonies of pleasant sound ; yet this gifted traveler was once an ignorant boy. Now he meddles with all knowledge, lives in all time, shares in all triumphs, and hopes for all good.   How important and delightful the work, and how wonderful and glorious the results, of polishing a rough diamond !

7

CHAPTER V.

BRILLIANTS.

DIAMONDS are known by a variety of names, according to the form in which they are cut, and the form is usually determined by the size and value of the stone. If the stone is quite thin in proportion to its breadth, it can only be cut into a rose or a table diamond. The table is considered the least beautiful mode of cutting, and is used to turn fragments and thin stones to some account. This diamond has a square central facet, surrounded by two or more series of four-sided facets, corresponding to the sides of the square. The róse diamond consists of a central eight-sided facet of small size, eight triangles, one corresponding to each side of the table, eight trapeziums next, and then a series of sixteen triangles.

But the most perfect and beautiful of all is the *Brilliant.* This diamond has at the center or top a principal face, called the table, which is surrounded by a number of sloping facets ; below it has a small face parallel to the table, connected by elongated facets with the edge of the upper part. The depth of a brilliant is nearly equal to its breadth, hence this diamond can only be cut from a thick stone. The facets of a brilliant are so formed as to powerfully reflect and refract the light, and if the stone is sufficiently rich when brought into a strong light it will dazzle the eye of the beholder with its glitter.

There are many more varieties of minds than there are of diamonds, these varieties consisting in part of inherent qualities, and in part of peculiar moldings received in systems of education and the habits of life. One cannot study the history of the great without being forcibly impressed that there is a wide difference in the processes and periods of development, even among those who attain to similar spheres of thought and action. Some are intellectual prodigies — brilliants — from birth, devouring books, and attempting composition in the nursery — springing almost from the cradle to realms of learning and fame ; while others, with benumbed intellects, grope on to manhood or middle life before their genius fully awakes, but even then attain to the celebrity of the others. We are aware that this term genius has been defined a thousand times, and in nearly as many ways. Some writers have considered it an intuitive and spontaneous power, denominating all trained ability mere "talent." But we think distinguished mental superiority, however acquired, deserves the title of genius. With some this is doubtless originally inherent, and, like the pinion of the eagle, rises immediately to strength, while with others it is developed by protracted and painful processes. The oratorical genius of Patrick Henry was original and spontaneous, bursting forth unexpectedly and volcano-like at the trial of the "Parson Cause" in Virginia; but with Demosthenes, Whitefield, Prentice, and Clay, it was the result of most assiduous cultivation. Who will say that the latter were not as deserving of the title as the former?

The poetic genius of Shakspeare was also spontaneous, his mind being poorly cultivated, and his plays the only literary attempts of his life; while the genius of Milton, displayed in

"Paradise Lost," was the opulent product of forty-five years of literary application.

Watt, Fulton, Morse, and Ericsson were certainly all geniuses, but their successful inventions resulted from the depth of their culture, and not from the spontaneous outburst of uncultivated imagination. And what less can be said of Franklin, Leverrier, Agassiz, and Audubon? Genius, then, comprises several varieties—may be brilliant and startling at the beginning, may quietly slumber for a considerable period, or require culture and training for its successful exercise.

The opinion has sometimes obtained that a precocious child either develops into a stupid adult, or, like a spring flower, fades early. Hence premature development has frequently been considered an irremediable calamity. A somewhat careful consideration of the subject has, however, convinced us that early death is by no means a necessary sequence of precocity, and that a genuinely brilliant child has seldom become stupid unless broken by disease, a misfortune (sometimes inherited, but oftener resulting from mismanagement or misconduct) which has eclipsed the career of far too many.

It is interesting to know how many distinguished authors and public men were precocious children, gleaming, almost from birth, with intellectual fire. Matthew Henry read the Bible aloud to his mother before he had completed his third year, and was familiar with the Greek Testament before he had passed his ninth. Timothy Dwight learned the alphabet at a single lesson, and read the Bible very distinctly before he was four years old. Hannah More in babyhood slipped through the incipiencies of her education no one knew how, and was reading fluently before her parents, who were instructing her older sisters, discovered it. Richard Watson at six years took up the study of Latin, and about the same age read eighteen volumes of general history, and hungered for more. Voltaire said he composed poetry in the cradle; and Dudley A. Tyng read mature Latin authors at six years, receiving at that period a prize copy of Virgil for his proficiency in reading it. Before Goethe was ten he wrote several languages, meditated poems, invented stories, and had considerable familiarity with works of art. Robert Hall at nine years was devouring "Butler's Analogy," "Edwards on the Will," and similar profound works. Pascal at thirteen was solving on stones in the street problems in geometry, though he had never seen a book on the subject. At sixteen he wrote an essay on Conic Sections, which the astute Descartes pronounced excellent. Isaac Newton, who was a dull boy, but a precocious youth, mastered the mathematics and philosophy of Descartes before he was twenty. Bacon at sixteen formed the plan of overturning the philosophy of Aristotle taught in the universities, and Edmund Burke at nineteen planned a refutation of the metaphysical theories of Berkeley and Hume. Calvin wrote his "Institutes" at twenty-five, which were a few years later enlarged, but not otherwise changed. Stillingfleet published his "Irenicum," his great work on Church government, at twenty-four ; and Grace Aguilar, the talented Jewess, published more than a dozen volumes, and died at thirty-one. Melanchthon received his bachelor's degree at Heidelberg at fourteen, at seventeen was Doctor of Philosophy, at twenty-one Professor of Ancient Languages, and at twenty-four published his most celebrated theological treatise, which he lived to see pass through seventy editions, and which

Luther declared worthy of a place among "canonical books." Dr. Andrew P. Peabody graduated at Harvard at fifteen years. Byron at twenty published his satire on "English Bards and Scotch Reviewers." Irving wrote for the press at nineteen, and at twenty-six issued his "Knickerbocker." Pope wrote his "Ode on Solitude" at twelve, his "Pastorals" at sixteen, and his "Essay on Criticism" at twenty. Macaulay wrote poetry of some merit. at fourteen. W. C. Bryant at ten penned poems which were printed in the country papers, and at nineteen completed his "Thanatopsis," considered by many the rarest gem of his gifted genius.

These examples show that a large number of illustrious persons were children of premature development, and instead of gliding into obscurity attained a celebrity far in advance of their years, and which they ever afterward maintained.

And it cannot be said that their genius or their literary undertakings necessarily abridged their career. Their term of years compared favorably with their less gifted and less literary contemporaries. Isaac Newton completed a very active and buoyant career at eighty-five;

Irving, though never well, lived on to seventy-seven ; and Hannah More, whose fertile genius never slumbered, attained her eighty-ninth year. Leibnitz died at seventy, Bolingbroke at seventy-three, Goethe at eighty-three, Voltaire at eighty-four, Edward Everett at seventy, and Humboldt at ninety years—all precocious children. Bryant is still hale at seventy-eight. Lord Bacon died at sixty-five, Burke at sixty-seven, Robert Hall at sixty-six, Pope at fifty-six, Calvin at fifty-five, and Matthew Henry at fifty-two. Richard Watson, who never saw a well day, died at fifty-two ; while Melanchthon, a gentle blue-eyed shadow, lived to be sixty-three. The profound Pascal fell at thirty-nine, the early victim of asceticism ; and the gifted Tyng at thirty-three, from a sad accident.

It is probable that Melanchthon, Calvin, Henry, Hall, Watson, Grace Aguilar, and others, represented by Fletcher, Pollok, and Henry Kirke White, shortened their days by incessant study and insufficient physical exercise. Mr. Fletcher's long-continued and oft-repeated fastings, his intense and incessant application to the pastorate, with his books and his pen, shunning every thing that savored of recreation, cast, on the one hand, a healthful reproof on the idle and voluptuous living of his time, but sapped prematurely the fountain of life, and abridged a most saintly and brilliant existence. Days of labor in the field occasionally, or of harmless sport in the forests, on the rivers and lakes, casting off all thoughts of toil and study, would probably have added bright and fruitful years to his earthly career. John Milton, Richard Watson, Kirke White, and many others, spent whole nights over their books notwithstanding the earnest protestation of friends, paying afterward the sad penalty which came in the form of enfeebled eyesight, nervous and debilitated constitutions, or an early death. Daniel Webster said he had "a genius for sleep," and if other brilliant minds had systematically cultivated this genius, not a few of them would have lived happier and toiled longer. Neglecting the development of their physical forces, their "intellects were to their bodies like hot fires which burn out the furnaces wherein they glow and blaze." It is also certain that another class, represented by Byron, who died at thirty-six, and Edgar A. Poe, who fell at thirty-eight, destroyed them-

selves, like the conqueror of the East, by recklessness and dissipation.

But while we have thus shown that this
brilliant premature development is not necessarily the prelude to an early grave, we do not
suppose that we have satisfactorily accounted
for the mediocrity of the masses of precocious
children. Those who rise to such eminence
as to have their names recognized in all the
world are to the masses, even of their own
class, as rich diamonds are to the sands upon
the shore. We doubt not the much larger
portion of prematurely brilliant children die
early, not a few of whom fall the unconscious
victims of parental ambition. Gifted with extraordinary capacity, they are pressed beyond endurance, and go down suddenly, like a shooting
star.

A precocious child should never be goaded
to study, but at times retarded and encouraged
to play. No one knows how, when, or where
such a child learns its lessons, but its recita-
tions are usually good. If there is an apparent
failure, it generally arises from an aversion
to systematic study, preferring to devour one
book, or master one science at a time, instead

of advancing with a class moderately into several. They not unfrequently wander outside of the regular course which they are expected to pursue, and often in this way lose laurels they might easily win. Richard Watson's great love of play, which his fragile frame so greatly needed, led his excellent mother to remind him of the length and difficulty of his classical studies, and the necessity of closer application, to which he invariably responded, " I can say my lesson." Fearing he was not sufficiently diligent she applied to his teacher, and found, to her surprise, that his progress was highly satisfactory. The mind of such a person gathers knowledge from books and nature like a sponge gathering water—literally sucking in all it touches.

Precocious and brilliant children have often appeared to their parents and teachers, who could not understand them, as obstinate and disobedient. With a deep-seated and all-controlling genius for science, poetry, navigation, art, mechanics, or literature, they have been unable to command any interest in the occupation or pursuits marked out for them by others. And no amount of admonition, or even forcible restraint from the legitimate bent of their minds, could dampen their aspirations. Petrarch's father, to insure the success of his son at the law, cruelly burned, in his presence and in spite of his screams and sobs, the poetical library he had industriously collected. But all this did not make the son a lawyer or prevent his becoming a poet. Alfieri was long delayed in the march of his genius by the misguided rigor of his uncle. Pascal was not allowed a book on higher mathematics, yet without a volume or a teacher he mastered the system of calculations which the books contained. Columbus was born a navigator, and no amount of discouragement could quench the ardor of his mind.

This principle is well illustrated by a tale in the romance of King Arthur. A poor cowherd is represented as coming to the king requesting that one of his sons be made a knight. "It is a great thing thou askest," responded King Arthur, who expressed himself anxious to know whether the request proceeded from the father or the son. Whereupon the old man replied, " Of my son, not of me ; for I have thirteen sons, and all these will fall to that labor I put them ; but this child will not labor for me for any thing that I and my wife will do, but always he will be shooting and casting darts, and glad to see battles, and to behold knights, and always, day and night, he desireth to be made a knight." The king becoming interested, ordered him to bring in all his sons. When they came he saw that twelve of them "were shapen much like the poor man; but Tor was not like any of them in shape or in countenance, for he was much more than any of them, so King Arthur knighted him."

In many families there springs up a little *Tor*, who in mind, purpose, and habit is quite unlike all the rest, and, because unlike them, he not unfrequently becomes a grief to his parents and others. He will not study law or medicine or follow the plow. If sent with a servant to the market to sell produce, like another genius he leaves the business with the servant while he departs to study mathematics or gather valuable information. Perhaps he is awkward or ill-formed, and of a retiring and somber disposition. Genius generally buds and blooms in solitude. Boyle, when a boy pursuing his studies, "would very often steal away from all company and spend four or five hours alone in the fields thinking at random." Alfieri tells us that nearly every evening after sea-bathing he seated himself on the beach behind a high rock, which concealed from his sight every part of the land behind him, while before and around him he beheld nothing but the sea and the heavens ; the sun sinking into the waves lighting up and embellishing these two immensities. He there passed many hours of delightful rumination. La Caille, who ranked among the first French astronomers of the last century, was the son of a parish clerk. When but ten years old his father made him ring the church bell every evening, but the family was much annoyed that his return from the church should be at such a late hour. Severe whipping did not secure his prompt return. It was finally ascertained that after ringing the bell he was in the habit of sitting down in the steeple and watching the stars. His father continued to punish him, though he knew the cause of his loitering in the steeple. His love of science, however, could not be suppressed. He lived to publish lectures on mathematics, mechanics, astronomy, and optics, which have passed through many editions.

In these silent musings the mind of the miniature poet revels amid gorgeous imagery ; the coming sculptor luxuriates amid forms of beauty ; the painter studies the ingenious blending of colors ; the musician dwells in the realms of sound ; the astronomer marks the appearance and progress of the stars ; and the philosopher communes with the intricacies of nature.

Some minds sweep through the most profound and intricate branches of study with the strength and speed of a tornado. All preliminaries and incipiencies are overleaped, and what others have labored years to solve is by them grasped in an instant. Isaac Newton having examined and comprehended the philosophy of all his predecessors by the time he attained his majority, began at once to sound the unknown, and at twenty-three invented his method of analysis for calculating, known as fluxions. Experimenting on the construction of a telescope he was led into an examination of the nature of light, and at twenty-four made known the corpuscular, or what has since ranked as the Newtonian theory. Discovering at the same time by a few experiments the error of Descartes in employing ground glass for lenses in the telescope, his mind instantly turned to the true theory, that of employing the reflecting lens, and after many experiments he completed at the age of twenty-six the first reflecting telescope ever made, and though it was only six inches long, it completely demonstrated the principles and theory he had conceived. Other minds had observed the pressure of solid bodies on the earth's surface, the tendency of bodies to fall when set free in mid-air, and the uniform movement of the planets, and numerous theories to explain the subject had been presented. Kepler, Archimedes, Galileo, Descartes, Gasendi, Leibnitz, Wren, Halley, and Hook had made approaches toward a proper solution of the subject ; but it remained for the mind of Newton to sweep deliberately through all their researches, retaining every thing valuable in the studies of each, and with experiment and mathematical demonstration set forth " the greatest scientific discovery ever made," the principle of gravitation, establishing the fact of the perfect identity of this force, whether marking the falling apple or the circling planet. His *Principia*, an elaborate work, covering his entire system of Natural Philosophy, and which

La Place, the greatest philosopher of France, assigned "a pre-eminence above all the other productions of the human intellect," was com-posed in the brief period of a year and a half. What others had toiled a score of years to investigate this brilliant genius comprehended in a day. He shrank from no investigations calculated to elucidate science, and every-where proved himself the superior of his associates, unraveling their theories, and brushing away their errors.

The late John M'Clintock, LL.D., considered eight minutes ample time to devote to the best filled daily journal, and his rapid intellect sped with equal velocity and ease through the most labored works of science and theology. In examining the works of others his attention skipped from point to point with the ease and grace of a bird in the air, yet he never overlooked any thing of importance. He could sit down in a strange room, carry on a conversation, and while another was arranging his toilet, glance so thoroughly through a new work he had picked up from the table as to close the volume and submit with credit to a close examination of its contents and merits. He would read a treatise and write a critical review while another was loitering at the outset. It was this power of rapid analysis which made him every-where and on all subjects such a bristling encyclopedia of knowledge and talent.

Some minds possess an ability for solving mathematical calculations which is truly surprising. The example of Truman Henry Safford is exceedingly striking. "After a very brief attendance at a country school in Vermont, with an attenuated frame and feeble health, this boy, at the age of nine years and six months, produced the 'Youth's Almanac for 1846,' having made all the calculations of eclipses, the rising and setting of the sun, etc., without any assistance." At the age of thirteen he also calculated without assistance the orbit of the telescopic comet of November, 1848, and his calculations agreed with those of the best astronomers. A gentleman went some years since to see and examine him with difficult problems. He says, "The interrogatories were of a very difficult nature, resolved mentally and according to rules of science, and generally with great instantaneousness. For the purpose of testing the reach of his mind in computation he was finally asked to multiply in his head 365,365,365,365,365,365 by 365,365,365,-365,365,365. He flew around the room like a top, and pulled his pantaloons over his boots, bit his hand, rolled his eyes in their sockets, until, in not more than one minute, said he, ' 133,491,850,208,566,925,016,658,299,941,583,-225.' What was still more wonderful, he began to multiply at the left hand, and to bring out the answer from left to right, giving first 133,491, etc.   Here, confounded above measure," says Mr. Paine, " I gave up the examination."

Here we have satisfactory evidence of the astounding fact, that a self-tutored boy multi-plied two sums, each composed of eighteen numerals, and stretching from units to quadrill-ions, in a minute of time, without slate or pencil, and gave the correct product.

Some brilliant minds, in addition to won-drous perception, have also possessed a memory so capacious and retentive that every thing brought to the attention has been distributed and laid up in its appropriate place. Themis-tocles could name all the citizens of Athens, amounting to twenty thousand. Cyrus knew the names of all the soldiers in his army, which

was also true of the Roman emperor Adrian.
Napoleon had a wonderful memory. Dr. Ley-
den could repeat any act of Parliament or similar document after a single reading. Pascal
remembered all he read and all he thought, and
Ben Jonson could at any time repeat, from
memory, every line he had ever written on any
subject. Sir Walter Scott repeated with accu-
racy a poem of twenty-eight stanzas which he
had heard but once sung, and that once occurred
three years before. A blind man in Glasgow
a few years ago could repeat the entire Bible
from Genesis to Revelation. Voltaire is said
to have once read a long original poem to the
king of Prussia. The king had ingeniously
placed a man of prodigious memory behind the
screen, where he could hear all and not be observed. When the reading ceased, the king
remarked that the production could hardly be
an original one, as there was an Englishman
present who could repeat every word of it.
The Englishman came forward and repeated it
word for word, to the astonishment of the poet,
who tore the manuscript in pieces, but on his
being made acquainted with the secret he was
glad to copy it again from the second repetition.

The late Alexander Von Humboldt is said to have possessed a memory that literally retained every thing. A gentleman just returned from a visit to an ancient city was describing to him some minute feature of the place, whereupon Humboldt corrected him, and the gentleman acknowledged promptly the error, and inquired "When were you there?"   "O," said Humboldt, "I have never been there, but fifty years ago I meditated making a trip to that place, and accordingly read the descriptions of the place to prepare myself."   So his mind had held the minutest description of an ancient city for fifty years so completely that he could correct the remark of one who had just examined it.

Edward M. Stanton, though a most industrious attorney and an indefatigable officer of the General Government, found time to cultivate general literature, and could repeat from memory whole volumes from the works of Charles Dickens. Fanny Crosby, the blind poetess of New York, informed the author that on one occasion, when under a contract to write a hundred poems for a music publisher, she composed and corrected forty-five of them, embracing a great variety of topics, before she called her amanuensis, and then dictated them all, at a single sitting, for the press.

We are not all *brilliants* in the sense that many of these were and are, at whose talents we have glanced in this brief chapter; but the fact that we are not affords no ground for discouragement or suspension of effort. Nearly all possess more ability than they are conscious of, and more than they employ. The powers of some bloom early, and those of others late. Some burst at once into glory and strength, while others mature through prolonged and painful processes. Disraeli has well said, "The natures of men are as various as their fortunes. Some, like diamonds, must wait to receive their splendor from the slow touches of the polisher; while others, resembling pearls, appear at once, born with their beauteous luster."

CHAPTER VI.

DIAMONDS OF THE FIRST WATER.

FOR ascertaining and expressing quality, a variety of methods has of necessity been introduced. The moral character of an individual is ascertained by comparing his inward experience and life-work with the requirements of the moral law, and the quality is expressed by such terms as truthful, pure, upright, righteous ; or by false, unholy, treacherous, wicked, etc. The precious metals when taken from the mines, and when employed in the arts, are seldom either found or employed in their unalloyed state. Hence, some method for ascertaining and expressing the true amount of pure metal which the admixture contains has been found necessary. Gold is reckoned by carats, which term the ancient Arabians borrowed from the Greek κεράτιον, which signified a little horn, or the fruit of the carob-tree, and is equal to four grains,

or four of the smallest particles employed in
weight. To ascertain the fineness of a gold
ornament, the whole mass is supposed to be
divided into twenty-four equal parts, and the
gold is reckoned in proportion as its substance
makes up the admixture, as ten, fifteen, twenty,
or twenty-two carats.

The weight of all precious stones is ascertained and expressed, like that of gold, in carats ;
but, unlike gold, the exact weight of a diamond
affords no estimate of its quality or value. The
quality of a diamond is always expressed by the
term "water," first water signifying first quality,
second water second quality, third water third
quality, etc. The most perfect diamonds are
entirely transparent and colorless, resembling
a drop of the purest water ; though colored
stones, where the color is evenly distributed
and the stone quite transparent, are also, as we
have elsewhere shown, highly prized.

While it is true that the beauty, the learning,
the estimate, and the apparent good in society
is largely superficial, there is still no consideration upon which all people lay such stress as
genuineness of *quality*. However deceitful and
treacherous the masses, no one is willing to take

a counterfeit. However largely a lady deals in false curls, false flowers, false words and charms, when she pays a large price for a diamond she is careful to secure a stone of the first water. And when that subtle deceiver, grown gray in his artful inventions, purchases a gold-cased chronometer, he is scrupulously anxious to ascertain just how many carats fine it is, and how many jewels enter into its machinery. Honesty, truthfulness, and purity, are what all people inflexibly demand of all others.

The qualities of some things are unchangeable, while those of others are susceptible of modification and improvement. As far as we know, the world of physics, including nature and art, is furnished with no method whereby the real quality of a diamond may be improved. Intense heat may dissipate the coloring, and the removal of the crust or the abrasion of its surface may disabuse the lapidary of erroneous impressions concerning its quality, yet no positive improvement in the quality of the stone is made. It must forever remain as nature formed it, of the first, second, or third water, or of a still inferior quality.

But the world of mind transcends the world

of matter, not only in the nature of its creations, but also in the facilities for improving the qualities of its creations. Though mind is invisible, impalpable, imponderable, it is still a positive essence, invested with a legion of forces, and capable of defection and remedy. In a previous chapter we have seen that the intellectual powers are capable of favorable transitions; and we hope to show in this that the moral qualities of the soul are also susceptible of radical transformations, changing the tenor of the life, raising man to higher usefulness, purer pleasures, and a nobler destiny.

All souls emerge into the realm of being in a lapsed or morally-discolored condition. For the sad cause of this we need not pause to inquire; the fact itself is patent, and almost universally conceded. The soul begins its career with an inborn love of evil, an imagination more or less distorted with an enfeebled and bewildered conscience, with decided leanings toward extreme selfishness, and with no true love to God, or just conceptions of its highest happiness.

It is a principle in philosophy that any thing set in motion will continue to move on in a given direction, unless some extraneous influence is brought to bear upon it. The tendency of every thing in nature is in keeping with this principle. It is the tendency of fire to burn, and to constantly increase the volume of its flame. It is the natural tendency of a fountain, or of a cataract, to continue to pour forth its waters. It is the tendency of a falling body to still fall, and increase its velocity as it passes through space. In like manner it is the tendency of the fallen soul to continue its downward wanderings, and, as the exercise of a power increases its strength, the faculties of a sinful mind are being continually hardened and intensified in evil, under accumulated guilt, and ever-increasing danger of deeper demoralization. It is on this principle that the smiling infant sometimes develops first into a rude boy, then into a vicious youth, and after a career of crime, growing blacker every revolving year, dies at length in prison or on the gallows, a blasphemous outcast. So, also, the charming maid, whose polished form, expressive eye, and enchanting tresses render her an object of attraction, tastes, at first sparingly, of forbidden pleasures until, demoralized, she loses shame, reeks in vice, and falls, a discolored mass of unsightly putrefaction.

Every soul becomes early conscious of its evil proclivities ; yet it fears them not, believing itself capable of holding them in check, and of employing them only at intervals and at pleasure. Scarcely any consider it likely that they shall descend to great evils, even with the freest indulgence. The rapid and appalling progress of indulged evil in the soul is very little considered by men, though all time has been strewn with the wrecks of humanity. The first impulse to lust, to thirst for power, and the early blush of youthful anger, appear harmless ; yet all history proves that these, when indulged, culminate in debauchery, tyranny, and in seas of blood. Cain little imagined what would be the end of the jealous feeling he first indulged toward his amiable brother. When Absalom, that gay and beautiful youth, the ornament of his family and the pride of Israel, first launched his perilous bark on a forbidden sea, he had no conceptions of the crimes that should forever crimson his soul and blacken his memory. Iscariot saw only the good in his covetousness until eternal disaster burst upon his affrighted soul. When James Gardiner forsook the home of his pious mother, he knew not the depths of profligacy to which his infatuated heart would lead him. Dr. Dodd did not expect to die a convicted forger, nor Dr. Webster a murderer. Arnold knew he was unscrupulous, yet he did not intend to be an open traitor. Kidd did not expect to be executed for piracy, nor Walker for filibustering. The moral diamond is sadly discolored, and so stealthy and fearful is the march of this blackening taint, and so impotent all natural remedies, that its perils are truly appalling.

Now, if these moral diamonds are universally found in a discolored condition, possessing no power of self-purification, but an invariable tendency to still greater defilement, then an extraneous method of moral recovery, containing every needed appliance, and adapted to all, was imperatively demanded. This, we believe, has been introduced by the Lord Jesus Christ. His person has been made the atoning sacrifice for human guilt, the only discolorment, which is instantly washed away when our faith accepts him. His example and law are set forth as the perfect rule of man's belief and practice, the

school for the education and guidance of his
conscience. The truths of this scheme are
entirely intelligible and within the scope of all,
equally interesting to all, while the influences
that attend them do affect and may be effica-
cious in transforming and purifying all.

Here, then, is the sublimest art in the universe of God, infinitely transcending all human
wisdom, and worthy of the profoundest study
and admiration of all the intelligences of earth
and heaven. In the laboratory of nature the
Infinite Artificer has foiled us. We cannot
number the ages, nor trace the processes by
which he elaborated the transparent gem from
its unsightly ingredients. But here his work,
though mysterious, is imperfect. Diamonds are
not all of the first water, and when one is discolored or fractured there is no remedy. Ages will
not purify or heal it. But in the world of mind
—"hear it, ye heavens, and be astonished,
O earth!"—in the world of mind so perfect and
all-powerful is his method that he takes the
most mangled, polluted, sin-blackened soul-gem
in the entire circle of humanity, and in an instant of time transforms it into a diamond of the
first water! The discolored becomes transpar-

ent, the sinner is made a saint, the demon of darkness is transformed into an angel of light and glory.

This transformation unites, and sublimely links, the soul to God. Man then becomes in a high sense a "partaker of the divine nature," which purifies his motives, ennobles his conduct, and opens new fountains of blessedness to his expanding soul. But however desirable this work to the Infinite Purifier, he never violates the principles of human liberty in its accomplishment. Though he convinces all of its importance, this state must be as distinctly and perseveringly sought as the exact knowledge of the stars, or the possession of the gems in the mine.

Through a vast variety of agencies, some of them the most simple imaginable, the benevolent Father seeks the awakening and recovery of his blinded offspring. Nature, providence, society, and the pages of written revelation, are alike rendered tributary and made vocal in this absorbing undertaking. Some are reached through the eye, others through the ear, and still others through the imagination. Some are awakened in the church, others in the solitudes of the forest; some amid the roaring of the storm on the boiling deep, and others amid the smiling of the landscape under a summer sky.

A pious sailor, who had spent nearly all his life on the sea, informed the writer that he never was profoundly impressed with the greatness of God and of his relationship to him until he was witnessing a *post mortem* examination. The sudden death of his comrade had not particularly impressed him ; but the ship surgeon resolved, if possible, to ascertain the cause. He laid open the casement that contained the vitals of the deceased youth, and as this hardened tar looked on and beheld the exquisite order and finish of that wondrous machinery, he was so overwhelmed with a sense of God's wisdom and goodness, and his own vileness, that he instantly resolved to reform, and became a decided Christian.

Some years ago a large institution of learning was destroyed by fire, scattering cinders and half-burned papers for a great distance around. A few days later a farmer, who had ignored religion all his life, began to plow in his field near the remains of the burned building. The day was warm. While resting his team he seated himself upon the beam of his

9

plow, and observing a scorched paper on the ground, he picked it up and read it again and again.　It was a leaf from that much neglected book, the Bible, which he would not have read in the house or in the field if he had known what it was.　His prejudice gave way, his heart bled, and not long after he told the affecting story of his awakening and wonderful recovery.

A countryman was crossing, on a hastily prepared skiff, a turbulent stream, greatly swollen with recent storms.　In the midst of the rushing current his frail bark went to pieces, and only with the most prodigious exertions was he enabled to regain the shore.　Impressed with the magnitude of his perils in those awful moments, and the infinite love of Him who had lifted him again to land, he fell upon the shore to bemoan his sins, and surrender his life to the matchless Redeemer.

Many years ago there resided in a thriving Connecticut village an intelligent young man, the chorister of a large church, but who had advanced into married life without personal piety.　In the early hour of a lovely spring morning he was standing on the bank of the Farmington River.　His eye glanced along its shelving banks, where leaflets nodded and glistened with the rising spray. He surveyed the distant mountain, with its towering peak and changing hues, over which the orb of day was just darting his sparkling light, tinging crag and cloud with golden drapery. Awed with the harmony and exuberance of this enchanting scene, his soul involuntarily exclaimed, " *There is a God, there is a God, and I am accountable to him!*" He returned to his house greatly exercised, and sought retirement in his room. He read his Bible, walked the floor, but found no rest. To pray seemed impossible, but he resolved to try. In walking the room his eye caught a mark on the floor, and he said, " At that point I will kneel and call upon God." Coming to the place, he fell upon his knees, and his agonized heart went out in strong desire, and soon an indescribable peace and sweetness filled his soul. He arose a renewed man. His experience became the key to his theology. Smitten with a sense of God's amazing and universal love to sinners, and burning with a desire to assist in saving them, he opened his doors to some pioneer itinerants, whose preaching and toils harmonized with his experience.

He became a life-long pillar in the new denomination, and left the odor of his piety long diffused in the community.

Colonel Gardiner was awakened in the slumbering visions of the night. Rejecting the counsels of his youth, he had descended by gradual processes to appalling depths of dissipation. Talented and vivacious in nature, he became the center and acknowledged prince of his profligate associates. But the lessons of his pious mother could not be obliterated. In the slumbers of the night the history of Calvary was illustrated to his imagination, and the voice of God spoke to his soul. Weeping and prayer followed, the Holy Spirit transformed him, and the "prince of profligates" became the prince among Christian soldiers. His former pleasures became the objects of deadly abhorrence. His biographer says : "I cannot but be astonished that he should be so wonderfully sanctified in body as well as in soul, as that from that hour (his conversion) he should find a constant disinclination to and abhorrence of those criminal sensualities to which he fancied he was before so invariably impelled by his very constitution that he was used strangely to think and to say that Omnipotence itself could not reform him without destroying that body and giving him another."

Two hours of the early morning of each day he invariably consecrated to religious reading and prayer. If the army marched at six he arose at four, and if at four, he arose at two, that the culture of his soul should not be neglected. He married, and became a most exemplary husband and father. Dr. Doddridge thought him the most deeply humbled and devout communicant that ever took the sacrament at his hand. One of his own letters to a friend exhibits the manner by which he prepared for that solemn service. After listening to a preparatory sermon on Saturday preceding the day for the Lord's Supper he says : " I took a walk on the mountains over against Ireland, and I persuade myself that were I capable of giving you a description of what passed there, you would agree that I had much better reason to remember my God from the hills of Port Patrick than David had from the land of Jordan, and of the Hermonites, and from the hill Mizar. In short, I wrestled some hours with the Angel of the Covenant, and made supplication to him with floods of tears and cries until I had almost expired ; but he strengthened me so that, like Jacob, I had power with God and prevailed. After such preparatory work I need not tell you how blessed the solemn ordinance of the Lord's Supper proved to me."

We have been explicit in sketching the history of this remarkable character that the reader may see that this discolored youth became unquestionably a diamond of the first water, and to disclose also the processes by which the wondrous change was effected.

But the loftiest triumphs of Christianity must be sought among tribes most benighted and imbruted. Geographers describe a group of about two hundred and twenty-five islands, great and small, situated between the fifteenth and twenty-second degrees of south latitude in the South Pacific Ocean, as the Fiji Islands. Of this group ninety-five are inhabited, and are estimated to contain a population of from two hundred thousand to three hundred thousand persons, divided into hostile tribes, ruled by a king and by subordinate chiefs. Though situated in a tropical region, endowed with the richest fruitfulness and the rarest embellishments of nature, these islands lay for many centuries entirely untouched by the civilization and Christianity of the world. Discovered by Tasman in the seventeenth century, and visited by Cook and Bligh in the eighteenth, the civilized world obtained no definite knowledge concerning them until within the last fifty years. Some early travelers had described these savages as a peaceful, happy, and somewhat virtuous people. About 1835 some English missionaries, with Bible in hand, entered this unknown field. With the climate and soil of the region they were completely charmed. The seeds of vegetables grew out of the soil in one day after planting, rare fruits and flowers covered the valleys and plains, and waved on the summits of the highest mountains ; but O how vile was man ! Every heart gloated in beastly enormity. Polytheism, polygamy, parent-murder, strangling of widows, infanticide, unstinted licentiousness, tyranny of woman, the horrors of inhuman and perpetual wars, all crowned with a dreadful passion for feasting on human flesh, which was frequently and horribly gratified. The inhabitants of one district had been from generation to generation preserved

simply as food for their more powerful neighbors, and were regarded as wild game fattening
for the market.   Husbands often baked and ate
their own wives.   The chief king of the islands
dwelt with his court on the island named Bau,
and had at least six ovens for roasting human
bodies, a score being sometimes cooked at a
time, and the ovens seldom allowed to grow
cold.

Into this vortex of shocking inhumanities,
this God-forsaken pandemonium of all fierce-
ness and brutality, these pious, brave men
entered to tell the story of redemption.   Establishing themselves as best they could, they
toiled on for the recovery of that people ten
years, amid difficulties, "abominations, and atroc-
ities" such as no pen can describe. ' In 1845
they were cheered with such a manifestation
of divine influence, sweeping over island after
island, such quickenings of the human conscience and melting of calloused hearts, such a
resurrection of exalted moral feelings, as have,
perhaps, never been excelled in the history of the
world.   All classes, from king to slave, melted
before it like wax in the fire.   "Business, sleep,
and food," said an eye-witness, "were almost

entirely laid aside," and some of the most atrocious characters that ever blackened the record of humanity were restored to virtue and purity. Chiefs of tribes that had mocked at all remonstrance in their career of butchery now quailed under the sound of exhortation and prayer. Varin, chief of Saru, long dreaded as the most inhuman butcher of his race, and whose sweep in crime had been too shocking to contemplate, broke down in agony of soul most intense and overwhelming. By earnest supplication to Jesus of Nazareth this dreadful murderer was transformed into a loving and amiable man, ready to preach the truths he once rejected and despised.

The capital of this barbarous empire was at length reached. Thakombau, the highest dignitary and king of all the Fijians, the head center of this carnival of human iniquity, enthroned in absolute dominion, feasting his wives and nobles on human flesh, was broken, as with a rod of iron, under the power of Christianity. After sorrow deep as his crimes had been enormous, after great humbling and crushing of his nature, he found peace, and stood up with uncovered head to confess his sins and glorify God before the chief men of his dominion.

"And," writes a missionary, "what a congregation he had! Husbands, whose wives he had dishonored ; widows, whose husbands he had slain ; women, whose sisters had been strangled by his orders, and whose brothers he had eaten ; and children, the descendants of those he had murdered, and who had vowed to avenge the wrongs he had inflicted on their fathers ! A thousand hearts heaved with astonishment and fear" as this dreadful man arose to speak in behalf of Christianity. His conversion was followed by that of the principal members of his court. The heathen temples were demolished, the sacred groves cut down, and where the cannibal-feast had usually occurred in the great square they erected a Christian church. Truly these moral transformations are the wonder of wonders in human society, if not in the whole universe.

But the finest purification and polish of this moral gem are not obtained in its first transformation from the power of evil. The measure and completeness of the work at that point vary in different individuals according to their amount of light, and the varying phases of their mental and moral constitutions. The work of grace in the soul is always characterized by gradations, its progress being dependent on the faith and obedience of the recipient. As with the natural diamond, so this gem passes through numerous advancing processes ere its purest brilliancy is displayed. The history of the queen of all the gems of England may, in a sense, illustrate the work of grace in the soul. That celebrated gem is said to have been obtained from the ruins of Golconda more than two thousand years ago. From the Rajah of Oojein it passed to the successive sovereigns of Central India, and in the fourteenth century was by Aladdin added to the treasures of Delhi. There it remained in the possession of the ruling families of the empire until the conquest of the Persians under Nadir Shah, who saw it glittering in the turban of the vanquished king, and by artfully proposing an exchange of head-dresses gained possession of the jewel, bore it away, and named it Koh-i-noor, or Mountain of Light. Some time after Nadir Shah was assassinated, and the diamond passed through the hands of Ahmed Shah of Cabool to Shah Soojah, who with it purchased his liberty from the conqueror Runject Singh, the " Lion of the

Punjaub," in 1813. In 1849 the Punjaub was
annexed to the territory held by the East India
Company, and a part of the stipulation was
that the renowned diamond should be surren-
dered to the Queen of England, and it accordingly came into her possession July 3, 1850.
When placed on exhibition in the Crystal
Palace of London in the following year, not a
few were disappointed that the glass model of
it should apparently excel the wonderful gem
itself. Its brilliancy only appeared when surrounded by a profusion of vivid lights, and without these it presented but a lusterless mass.
Its defects, however, arose from its imperfect
polish. It had been cut by its savage owners,
according to the style of India, into a table
diamond, the style least adapted to the full display of its excellence. After due deliberation it
was intrusted to Mr. Costar, the distinguished
Jewish lapidary of Amsterdam, with instructions
to bring it to its highest perfection, and his
experienced workmen converted it into a brilliant, successfully removing every blemish, since
which it has ranked among the rarest jewels of
the world, excelling alike in purity and fire.

Now, every marked transition through which

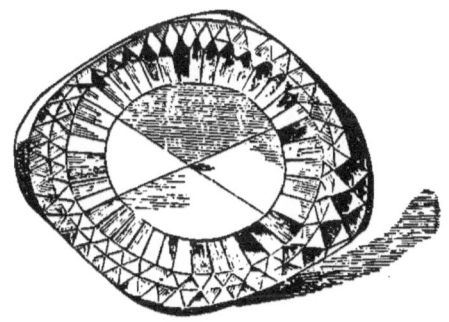

As cut in India over 2,000 years ago.

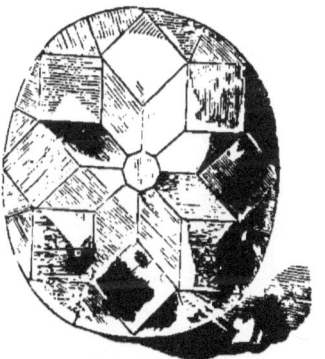

Front view: as recut by Mr. Costar.

Back view as recut.

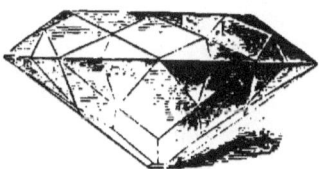

Side view as recut by Mr. Costar.

this jewel passed was an improvement, and at each time it was supposed by its possessors to have been brought to its highest perfection. Washing away the dirt that had for thousands of years concealed its luster in the mine was decided progress. Cutting it into a table diamond, exhibiting a large, brilliant surface surrounded by a hundred tiny facets, was a vast improvement on its entire past, and the diamond-cutters of India thought its glory completed. In this state it remained for centuries, until the scientific appliances at Amsterdam advanced it immensely beyond all that had gone before.

So every advance in the work of grace is a decided triumph, affording a better exhibition of humanity, and is mistakenly supposed by some to be very nearly the climax of human excellence. When John Bunyan had abandoned his grossest immoralities, and contracted the habit of attending church, he concluded he had attained the summit of all pious ambition, and boldly declared that he could now "please God as well as any man in England." The tribes of Israel found the land so much better on the eastern bank of the Jordan than it had been

in the wilderness of Sin that they foolishly concluded to remain there.   But it was better with
those who, having crossed the Jordan and conquered Jericho, passed on to Ai, and then to
Gibeah, and rested not until they ate the rich
fruits in the heart of the land.   That sublime
transformation, when the human jewel emerges
from the miry pit, takes rank among the gems
of God, exhibiting the first moral brilliancy of its
wondrous nature, vastly excels every thing that
has gone before, and in the raptures of the hour
the triumph seems complete.   But subsequent
cleansings and baptisms, with the frictions
attending a toilsome and often perilous career,
greatly intensify its brilliancy.   Edward Payson
experienced during the last weeks of his life,
and when nearly paralyzed in body, such revelations of divine grace as he had never experienced during the twenty years of his fruitful
ministry.   He exclaimed, "God is able to make
Christians happy without any thing else.   I am
a cripple, and not able to move, yet I am happier than ever I was before in all my life, or
ever expected to be ; and if I had believed this
twenty years ago I might have been spared
much anxiety."

Thoughtful experience proves that there are no intellectual or moral elevations attained which are not overtopped by other dazzling summits beyond, affording new incitements to the ascending soul. And whatever of apparent error, springing from unavoidable infirmity, may here seem to mar the transparency of this gem, it will be lost in its translation to the richer spheres of the Eternal. When His fashioning hand shall have brushed the last blemish from the jewel and its setting, and in a higher sense than before it is again said in heaven, "Behold, the man is become as one of us," it will fully appear that he is indeed *a diamond of the first water.*

CHAPTER VII.

SECLUDED JEWELS.

HE world is not so much the exhibition of great, as it is the aggre-
gation of small things. It is not
the great mountains that make its
surface ; nor the mammoth trees that
make its forests ; nor the great fortunes
that make its commerce ; nor the great
jewels that constitute its treasures. The
great things have their mission and place,
but reckon only as a small part of the
whole. The grandest mountains run in
isolated ranges, the mammoth trees stand in
separate groups, the princely fortunes look
down on seas of poverty, and the rarest diamonds are so few in number that their names
are easily remembered. If only the educated
read the volume, the circulation is limited ;
and if only the millionaires purchase the imported wares, the demand is small. Knolls,
hills, plateaux and plains make up the most

useful portions of the earth's surface, leaving the occasional peak as a part of nature's esthetic trimming of the locality, a bold and striking freak of creative skill. The rolling billows of the mighty deep with all their strength display only the blue, while all the colors of nature are seen in the scattering drops from the cloud. Great rivers are splendid as they wind their silver currents around the base of the mountains, and sweep on in silent grandeur to the ocean ; but the hillsides and plains must be fertilized by a thousand trickling rills, and moistened by innumerable showers, or all will come to desolation. The culmination of a great event is observed and chronicled by all, yet a hundred thousand silent, incipient steps led to the important result. Trivial things are important, and small matters potent, as well as those considered great. The igniting of a spark has led to a conflagration, the utterance of a thought to a revolution, the removal of a pebble to the rush of an avalanche.

And what is true in the world of matter is true also in the world of mind. The great discoverers, inventors, and reformers comprise but an insignificant fraction of general society.

10

The great philosophers study out the sciences, but millions of ordinary minds must take them up and teach them to the masses, or little practical benefit will result to the world. The great navigators explore the seas and discover the islands, but they must be followed by armies of plain, industrious colonists before civilization can rear her domes and conduct her schools and commerce. The greatest military chieftain is wholly impotent unless supplied with battalions and munitions. The great Reformers fearlessly uttered the truths, and set the example, but the Reformation resulted mainly from the toils and prayers of many thousand obscure persons, who preached the doctrines through the factories, workshops, and kitchens, and sung the poetry on the farm and around the fireside. Diamonds glittering alone in the mountain cliff are none the less gems, though no human eye has been dazzled with their brilliancy. Rich fruits often grow on neglected plains, and flowers of exquisite beauty bloom in secluded glens, whither no human being comes to admire their colorings or inhale their fragrance. So all the rarest qualities of the soul bud and bloom in solitude and in the humblest walks of life. Merle D'Aubigné, in his "History of the Reformation," has proven that Protestantism existed before the Reformation, and was often during the dark ages stronger than the Papacy. The Pope and his adherents could only maintain their corrupt tenets and practices by a perpetual slaughter of the lovers of truth, who inveighed against their abominations. Obscure men and women in the privacy of their own homes, and in monasteries, waited in genuine simplicity and faith on the true God, "lifting up holy hands without wrath o: doubting." Some talked of their experience in the deep things of God, and when hurled into prison, wrote out their confessions, hiding them in holes in the wall, some of which were not discovered until centuries afterward. Luther had a few earnest supporters among the great, but he had thousands of them among the plain and unpretentious. The Elector's protection was a valuable boon in his perilous work ; but the hungering of the thousands of plain men for the Word of God, their hearty reception of the truth, and the sublime exemplifications of their faith, were among his most important auxiliaries.

Speculations and heresies originate with the profound or the brilliant, whose talents only could give them currency ; but the plain people, who constitute the masses in all countries, are eminently conservative, and do not easily drift from their habitual moorings. The Germans of this century are a striking example of this truth. A few of their scholars, turning abruptly away from the traditional habits of their countrymen, are trying to open a new channel of thought for themselves and their brethren. The Germans have long been characterized by an excessive belief in the supernatural and marvelous. Instead of guarding against excessive credulity, these theorizers have boldly undertaken to sweep away every thing that savors of the supernatural, even the Bible itself. Happily, their books are read by a few of their own class only, the masses of the people taking no interest in them whatever. Extensive revivals of religion occur, in which thousands are converted, who toil under the shadow of the university, which is the center of rationalism and infidelity.

The world is perhaps as deeply indebted to the influence of those who toil unheralded in secluded circles as to the geniuses who occupy more conspicuous spheres. The modest, silent influence of a gifted and true woman has ten thousand times laid the foundation for brilliant public achievements ; and the secret influence of a woman has ruined multitudes. The influence of a mother vastly outmeasures all others in the molding of society. No matter what her faith, her conduct, her character, the bent of her mind, or the laws of her household, her power is supreme and well-nigh unlimited. Humanity is cast into her lap to be nurtured and fashioned for time and eternity. If elevated and saintly in mind and life, she lifts her offspring sublimely heavenward. Misguided, prejudiced, or imbruted, she is still mother, the supreme priestess of the circle, planting in the deepest soil of the soul seeds that must germinate into a harvest of crime and interminable woe.

The mother has vastly the advantage of the father in molding the mind of the child. His influence is occasional, hers unremitted. He must provide for the hive, hence his mind is absorbed with business, and with occupations lying wholly outside the nursery, while the highest ambition and glory of a true woman are linked to the success of her children. Home is her empire, where she rules much of the time without a rival. That a pious woman is sometimes opposed and baffled in her toil by a wicked and dissipated husband we all know, yet it will be difficult to find the example where prudence and piety ruled the mind of the wife and mother, who did not in the end conquer.

Nothing on earth is so fruitful in the formation of character, and creates so much happiness or misery, as the nature of one's home; and home takes its character chiefly from the matron who presides there. One thing is clear, *man cannot make home.* He can build the house, purchase the furniture, gravel the walks, plant the shrubbery, but it is still the veriest desert of gloom without the attractions of woman; and unless she who is called to fill it is a being worthy of the name, it is a dismal Sahara ever afterward. Occasionally one rises in after years above the atmosphere of his early home, but the vast majority breathe it to their lives' end. Some men desert an unpleasant home, though usually for something worse; but little children cannot desert it, and all its conversation, tempers, habits, and management enter into their education and assist in the formation of their characters. It is no wonder that girls are thoughtless and young men vile whose early years were spent in disordered homes, where foul speech, profanity, the clashing of evil tempers, dissipation, and uniform disregard of God were the general rule. How can a bad mother rear good children? and who can correct them when she has finished their education?

Girls more generally inherit the qualities of their fathers, and boys of their mothers. Jacob, the supplanter, was the complete daguerreotype of his mother Rebekah. Her counsels were seldom for a moment questioned, and never rejected. Every deceptive spark from the maternal steel produced a speedy and reciprocal flash in the mind of her boy. Walter Scott's mother was a superior woman, highly educated, and a great lover of poetry and painting. The mother of Byron was haughty, ill-tempered, and violent, and her bad qualities were all sadly perpetuated in her gifted son. The mother of Napoleon I. was distinguished for beauty and energy. He once said: " I owe principally my subsequent elevation to the manner in which my mother formed me at an early age." He also adds : " My opinion is, that the future good or bad conduct of a child entirely depends upon the mother." Lord Bacon's mother was noted for superior intellect and deep piety. The mother of Nero was a murderess, and what better could have been expected of her son ? Washington's mother was gifted and true. John Wesley was reared by a mother remarkable for the very qualities that rendered her son illustrious. The mother of the present generation of Beechers was a lady of great piety and worth. Her whole soul was enlisted in the training of her children. Many years ago, when residing on the east end of Long Island, she made this significant entry in her diary : " This morning I arose very early to pray for my children, especially that my sons may be ministers and missionaries of Jesus Christ." After a life of toil she died in great peace, but the Church has witnessed the conversion of her eight children, and has ordained her five sons to the Christian ministry. The mother of the younger Tyng was distinguished for force of character and mighty faith in God.

When gasping for breath on her dying bed her husband expressed anxiety about the children, to which she promptly responded, " My dear, give yourself no uneasiness about my children, God will bring them all to himself; that is his covenant with me." They were long since added to the Church of God. Bishop Watson believed that he inherited religious feelings from his excellent mother. Was not the same thing true of Jonathan Edwards, Timothy Dwight, John and Charles Wesley, Edward Payson, Archibald and William J. Foss, Alfred Cookman, and many others whose lives were brilliant ornaments in the world, reflecting also the highest honor on those that reared them ?

When you see a young man with an open, frank countenance — one elegant in manners, brilliant in mind, correct in his intercourse among men—you may safely conclude that he had a pure, loving, high-minded mother. The luster of a great jewel has been beaming upon him from the earliest dawn of his being. His infant slumbers were perhaps under the roof of a hovel, but the great heart that throbbed against his temples was purer and richer than the diamond. He is attracted by the beautiful in nature and art both by sight and sound, because his mother was alive to it and encouraged this propensity in her child. He sees a moral sublimity in honest industry, self-sacrifice, fortitude, and intelligent devotion to the true God because these sentiments were breathed in the atmosphere of his early home, and illustrated by the blaze of a daily example. That mother's influence will never be lost. After living, like the diamond in the sand, unnoticed, she may fall early and molder in an obscure grave, yet the germs she has planted in the mind of her boy will live and thrive. Every thing exquisitely modest or benevolent or kind or pure he meets in all his life will remind him of his mother, and touch a delicate chord in his soul that will never cease its vibrations.

How many glittering diamonds shine in the seclusions of the nursery and the sick-room! Shut in from the gayeties of general society, from the bustling scenes of the outside world, and often from the public sanctuary, they toil unnoticed over a precious charge through weary years. But she that weaves garlands of precious thoughts and hangs them in the gallery of an infant soul shall never lose her reward. To instruct that little motherless girl and soothe the sorrows of that crippled boy are matters which He that sitteth in the heavens will observe and take pains to reward. Especially let no mother feel that her work in seclusion can remain unnoticed or be unimportant. She toils in retirement, but time and eternity will reveal the nature of her exertion to the everlasting shame or glory of her that labors. In that infant form slumber the germs of powers that shall rise to strength and unceasing importance. The thoughtless observer may think it "a slight thing to clasp those tiny hands in prayer," and lead that opening mind in thought and song ; "yet few scenes on earth are more truly sublime," or fraught with more weighty results. That hand may yet grasp the scepter that sways an empire ; that voice may address unnumbered thousands on earth, and sing among the archangels in heaven ; that mind may yet decide a nation's policy, and explain the mysteries of eternity ; "that soul shall thrill through everlasting ages with the bliss of heaven," or writhe amid the endless torments of hell. Can any thing be considered small or unimportant that enters into the solution of so vast a problem?

A young woman sat thoughtfully in a little home in the city of New York. She was beautiful in person, accomplished in mind, and saintly in life. She had been reared in a cultivated family, and, though possessed of talent, learning, and dignity sufficient for a queen, she entertained sensible views of life, and chose to become the wife of an intelligent and pious mechanic. Several years roll pleasantly away, and as we find her again there is a brilliancy in her eye, a hectic flush upon her cheek, and a hollow cough that talks a language we cannot misunderstand. She is the mother of a beautiful boy, who has inherited her own versatile nature, and as he comes in from the street she hears him utter the name of Jesus in an irreverent manner. This is to her a matter of deep solicitude, and as her husband returns from his toil, she speaks of this circumstance with deep emotion, and inquires, "What shall we do to save our dear boy?" Her husband replies, "Well, my dear, we cannot shut him in entirely from the street; his little form needs exercise; we must teach him better, and pray for him as we

have done ; that is all that we can do." Weeks
pass, and one day as her husband returns from
his toil he finds his wife very weak, lying on
the bed ; but she murmurs not, and thinks not
of herself. Her first words are, " Husband, I
think I have hit upon a plan that will save our
boy. We will teach him a passage of Scripture
each day, and we will carefully select those pas-
sages that contain the name of Jesus, and in
this way I think he will learn to reverence the
Saviour." The pleasant task was at once be-
gun and continued until her early death.
When she felt the cords of life unbinding she
called him to her bedside, and, taking his hand
in hers, she said, " My dearest boy, your mother
is going to die, going to heaven. I want you
to promise her that you will continue this practice of committing the Scriptures through life ;
pray every day to God, and never under any
circumstances take the Saviour's name in vain."
His little breast heaved, his lip quivered, and
his voice faltered, yet he made the solemn
promise. Years have passed since this touching scene occurred, yet the promise of that
hour has not been forgotten. That boy is now
a studious, prayerful youth, and his father said

to us not long since, "I think his mother has anchored him to the throne." Queens have had more earthly splendor, more notoriety and fame than this saintly young woman, but if during her brief sojourn on earth she "anchored" the soul of that brilliant boy to the throne, has she not accomplished more than many a queen? Toiling in her modest way in her own chosen retirement, unheralded and unseen by the great, bustling world, who does not perceive that she was still a brilliant jewel?

But woman's influence is not confined to the nursery, nor does it operate solely in the capacity of a mother. As a sister, friend, and companion, she fills a sphere of almost infinite importance. How the gentleness and sunshine of an amiable sister quiets the turbulence of a family of boys. She is a jewel from which they all gather luster. The occasional presence and correspondence of a virtuous and esteemed lady friend has often quickened to lofty sentiments and purposes, and saved from discouragement and dissipation. How many clergymen, statesmen, and authors owe half their usefulness and success in life to their noble wives?

We know there have been many doleful chapters truthfully written on the domestic infelicities of men of genius. We cannot doubt that science, literature, religion, and all the purest interests of society, have often suffered because a vain, haughty, indiscreet, or uncultivated woman was wedded to the philosopher, the poet, the clergyman, or the statesman. Socrates had Xanthippe for his wife, a woman as crooked in nature as in name. The wife of Bishop Cooper in a freak of passion ruthlessly consigned to the flames the manuscript for his Lexicon, over which that industrious student had toiled many years. Whitelock's wife destroyed many of his valuable papers. John Milton was a mighty man at blank verse, but really weaker than ordinary men in arranging matrimonial alliances. His domestic infecilities were numerous and long continued. Perhaps these unhappy examples had their influence in leading Newton, Locke, Leibnitz, Bayle, Hobbes, Hume, Gibbon, Smith, Boyle, Voltaire, Pope, Cowper, Goldsmith, Michael Angelo, Lamb, Akenside, and Arbuthnot to decide in favor of celibacy.

But marriage, where prudence and affection

are blended, is no obstacle to the best attainments with either of the sexes, and our literary bachelors ought to know that Xanthippe died thousands of years ago, and has never had a resurrection. Married men more frequently than bachelors rise to celebrity. The inspiration imparted by a virtuous and gifted woman has nerved many a man in defeat ; her patience has quieted the turbulence of his breast ; her intuitive perception discovered the malady that was wasting his soul, and promptly suggested a remedy, and when all the world was dark and forlorn her sympathy has afforded a refuge and a solace. When a boy we read Irving's touching essay entitled " The Wife," and wept over it. We have read it again and again in later years, and always to weep and feel improved. Our observation coincides with his, that "a married man falling into misfortune is more apt to retrieve his situation in the world than a single one, partly because he is more stimulated to exertion by the necessities of the helpless and beloved beings who depend upon him for subsistence, but chiefly because his spirits are soothed and relieved by domestic endearments, and his self-respect kept alive by finding that,

though all abroad was darkness and humilia-
tion, yet there is still a little world of love at
home, of which he is the monarch. Whereas a
single man is apt to run to waste and self-neg-
lect, to fancy himself lonely and abandoned,
and his heart to fall to ruin like some deserted
mansion for want of an inhabitant." We, too,
as did that gifted author, have often had occasion to remark the fortitude with which women
sustain the most overwhelming reverses of fortune. "Those disasters which break down the
spirit of a man and prostrate him in the dust
seem to call forth all the energies of the softer
sex, and give such intrepidity and elevation to
their character that at times it approaches to
sublimity. As the vine, which has long twined
its graceful foliage about the oak, and been
lifted by it into sunshine, will, when the hardy
plant is rifted by the thunderbolt, cling round
it with its caressing tendrils, and bind up its
shattered boughs, so is it beautifully ordered
by Providence that woman, who is the mere
dependent and ornament of man in his happier
hours, should be his stay and solace when smitten with sudden calamity, winding herself into
the rugged recesses of his nature, tenderly sup-

11

porting the drooping head, and binding up the drooping heart."

A young American woman, reared in affluence, married early against the wishes of her friends, and removed with her husband to a large city. In a few months he was prostrated with disease, which rendered him a helpless invalid for life. Poverty soon stalked through their modest apartments. What was to be done? She had little knowledge of business, had not been inured to toil; but she was too brave to be discouraged. She began to ply the needle, but for many days received only six cents per day for ten hours' toil, with which she purchased a loaf of bread, on which, with a cup of water, they entirely subsisted. Seventeen long years, with unflagging exertion, she paid the large demands of householders, purchased medicines, reared an only child, consuming the midnight hour in painful endeavors to keep famine from her door, and then paid for an expensive burial of the remains of him to whom she plighted her early affection. During all those years she was so occupied in providing subsistence, and in ministering to her invalid companion and her child, that she never entered

a church or visited a friend ; yet she murmured
not, and would not acknowledge herself weary
or disappointed with life. Was she not a jewel?
The Marquis de Lafayette was one of the noblest
men of France ; but it must never be forgotten
that through all his deepest trials and sufferings
he was unwaveringly supported by a heroic
wife of solid piety and culture. She nobly ad-
hered to his principles when it cost the sacrifice
of splendor, of friendships, of family comforts,
and of life itself. Liberated from the prison at
Paris, where she had suffered, in ignorance of
her husband's fate, more than a year and a half,
and in feeble health, she was inflexible in her
determination to find the Austrian dungeon
and carry such consolation as she was able to
the wounded spirit of her persecuted husband.
Sending her son across the waters to President
Washington for safety, with her two daughters,
just blooming into womanhood, she crossed in
disguise the Austrian frontier, forced her way
into the presence of the emperor, and when she
could not obtain the liberation of her husband,
demanded the privilege of sharing his captivity.
To the filthy dungeon of Olmutz she bravely
descended to share the sorrows of the choice

of her youth. In this dreary vault of darkness and woe she lingered twenty-two months, contracting disease which broke her constitution, and she went down in the meridian of her life. She died in her forty-seventh year, but had lived long enough to exemplify virtue, generosity, patriotism, love of liberty, and piety. She trained her offspring to virtue and heroism. Her biographer pronounced her "the soul of her numerous family, the support of the poor, the ornament of her country, and the honor of her sex."

Martin Luther had, in his genial and noble-minded " Lord Kate," as he familiarly termed her, a mine of inexhaustible moral wealth. He uttered what a great many other men have felt when he said, "I would not exchange my poverty with her for all the riches of Crœsus without her." He said, "The utmost blessing that God can confer on a man is the possession of a good and pious wife, with whom he may live in peace and tranquillity."

Sir William Hamilton would probably have failed as Professor of Logic and Metaphysics in the University of Edinburgh had not his wife heroically supported him, toiling with him on numerous occasions all night on the preparation of a lecture he was to deliver the following morning. Many a blind advocate and minister has consulted books through the eyes of his wife, without which he would have been impotent, if not speechless.

We have read of women leaving their firesides and their children, searching the snow-covered prairies for many miles in search of their perishing companions, swooning with joy on finding them alive. They have gone to the bloody battle-field and carried away in their arms, amid the iron hail, the bleeding forms of those they loved, and from whom they could scarcely be separated. More than one has gone to the prison-cell and exchanged habits with her life-companion, that he thus disguised might pass the guard and once more breathe the air of freedom, leaving her to bear the rigor of prison treatment. Immense fortunes have been expended to find the remains of a shipwrecked companion. The wife of John Rogers followed him with all her children to his execution, supporting him with her presence and prayers in his dying agony. How many ministers would have hopelessly broken down in their toils and

privations had it not been for the Christian fortitude of their excellent wives? How many
thousands of men now esteemed *good* and *true*
would, under pressure, have abandoned their
principles, changed their habits, and abolished
their family religion, but for the fact that they
knew their wives would never surrender? As
the sills and foundation-stones, which are quite
concealed, in a cathedral are just as important
as the arch or tower, so these silent and invisible
influences are useful in molding and upholding
society. The conclusion of the wise man is,
"Whoso findeth a wife findeth a good thing,
and obtaineth favor of the Lord."

Woman is usually an angel of mercy, and
rarely sinks so low as to have no tears to shed
over the unfortunate and suffering. Her sym-
pathies are disinterested, wide as the world,
and lasting as her being. The little Jewish
maid, torn from her early home, and made a
slave in the palace of Naaman, forgot all resent-
ment in her desire to have her new master
cured of his leprosy. The finest feelings have
often manifested themselves among the women
of savage tribes. The well-told story of Poca-
hontas, the Indian girl of Virginia, intercept-

ing the deadly blow from the white man by the interposition of her own naked head, if true, is a striking example.

Mungo Park, a Scottish traveler, and one of the early explorers of Africa, gives in his journal one of the most touching instances on record. After suffering a tedious imprisonment in the capital of one of the barbarous tribes, confined in a room with a wild boar, he made his escape. Some time after in his wanderings he struck the Niger at Sego, a considerable city lying on both sides of the river. Communication with its different parts was kept up by large canoes, which were constantly crossing and recrossing. The crowd of passengers was great, and Park waited two long hours for an opportunity to cross, but was then disappointed, as orders came from the chief forbidding him to pass over. Hungry, dispirited, and faint, far from home and succor, in the midst of a strange land filled with barbarians and wild beasts, he turned, in the midst of a dreadful storm, under the boughs of a tree to spend a doleful night. But his moan attracted the ear of a poor negro woman returning from her toil in the field. With the instincts of a true woman she conducted him to her miserable hut, gave him food, and spread a mat on the floor as an apology for a bed, on which he was invited to sleep. There were several in the family, and the females continued their toil of spinning cotton till late at night. Their labor was interspersed with song, and one of the young women composed and sung one for the benefit of the suffering stranger. Literally translated it ran thus :

"The wind roared, and the rain fell;
The poor white man, faint and weary,
Came and sat under our tree;
He has no mother to bring him milk,
No wife to grind his corn."

Then came the chorus, in which they all joined with a sweet and plaintive air :

"Let us pity the poor white man,
No mother has he."

Park declared that no incident in his travels or his life so affected him. He was so smitten with this unexpected kindness that his weary, weeping eyes refused to sleep ; and when he departed in the morning he cut two brass buttons from his waistcoat and gave them to his sable benefactress, the only recompense he was ever able to confer.

How many brilliant little diamonds glitter in nomes of poverty, scattered through the hamlets, and amid the solitudes of the backwoods. Their thoughts and tones are richer and fairer than their cheeks, their tempers and examples sweeter than the odor of roses. Clad in coarse garments, and trained to self-denial, not corrupted by the flatteries or luxuries of the world, they live to Him that redeemed them, the joy of their parents, shedding the luster of their piety on all around them. Such were Elizabeth Walbridge, the Dairyman's Daughter, and Little Jane, the Young Cottager, whose histories have been so beautifully written by Legh Richmond.

The daughter of a French prisoner, though in feeble health, followed on foot over a hundred leagues the carriage that conveyed her father to prison. For months she toiled incessantly to procure his release, but died of over-exertion soon after his discharge.

When Gustavus III., King of Sweden, was one day riding on horseback through a village near his capital, he saw an interesting peasant girl drawing water near the roadside. As he was thirsty, he alighted and asked her for a drink. With artless simplicity and kindness she lifted the pitcher to the lips of the monarch, who, having satisfied his thirst, courteously acknowledged her politeness, and becoming more and more interested in her, said,

"My girl, if you would accompany me to Stockholm I would endeavor to provide you a more agreeable situation."

"Ah, sir," replied the girl, "I cannot accept your proposal. I am not anxious to rise above the state of life in which the providence of God has placed me ; but, even if I were, I could not for an instant hesitate."

"And why?" inquired the king, a little surprised.

"Because," answered the modest girl, "my mother is poor and sickly, and has no one else to assist or comfort her under her many afflictions ; and no earthly bribe could induce me to leave her, or to neglect the duties which affection requires me to perform."

"Where is your mother?" inquired the monarch.

"Yonder in that little cabin," replied the girl, pointing to a wretched hovel not far away.

The king entered, and found on a rude bedstead, covered only with a little straw, an aged

woman weighed down with infirmities and sufferings. Moved at the sight, he said feelingly,

" I am sorry, my poor woman, to find you in
so destitute and afflicted a condition."

" Alas, sir," she responded, " I should be indeed to be pitied had I not that kind and
attentive girl, who labors to support me, and
omits nothing she thinks can afford me relief."
And then, wiping away a tear, she added, " May
a gracious God remember it to her for good ! "

Noble, noble girl ! fairest, brightest jewel of
the realm ! she could not be attracted from the
hovel of her suffering mother by all the splendors of a king. Gustavus was so touched with
her constancy that he left a purse of money, and
shortly afterward settled on her a pension for life.

A pious lad in a New England town, attending the district school, felt a rising desire to do
good to his playmates. Accordingly he an-
nounced that there would be a prayer-meeting
in the school-room at noon during the inter-
mission. Some of the scholars laughed, and
jeered at his meetings, but others were awakened and wept. Some of the parents hearing
of the little noonday meeting attended, and
were deeply wrought upon. Then the ministers

of the place came in and assisted, and over sixty were hopefully converted. Was not that lad a little jewel?

These secluded jewels are found every-where, among both sexes, in high life and low, on sea and land. A reckless young man forsook the home of a pious mother, and resolved to be an infidel. He lived as if he had no soul to culture and save, and madly said in his heart, "There is no God." Dissipated and daring, to escape his friends and all religious influence he went to sea as a sailor. But lo! the captain of the vessel was a pious man. Every day he assembled the crew, read to them the Scriptures, and offered prayer. When the captain's eye glanced from the book to the little audience, the young man thought it pierced his inmost soul. Day after day he trembled under a load of guilt until it became intolerable, when he ventured to unburden his mind to the captain. The captain took him to his room, wept tears of joy over him, told him the story of Calvary, encouraged and trained him in piety, and finally returned him to his mother a reformed and converted young man. Are not such captains the rarest pearls of the sea?

Some wonder what people are, what those think, and how those feel who dwell a great many steps down the ladder of society below themselves. Now the truth very likely is, they think, and feel, and desire, and aspire, and hope very much like all the rest of the world. Perhaps they have more knowledge or sense on some points than we, perhaps less. Their sorrows, and joys, and fears do not greatly differ from ours. There are gems of exquisite polish often found far down among the poor and the lowly. A clergyman in New York city passing down a busy street encountered a sooty, noisy chimney-sweep. He had often seen such men, and heard their noise, and thought them a miserable, hopeless class in society. Curiosity and pity prompted him to more carefully inspect the stranger. Drawing near to him, he said,

"My friend, this must be a hard life that you live."

"Hard?" said the sweep. "O no, sir!" his eye brightening as he spoke; "life has its joys, and when it is over we shall go to rest."

"Do you ever go to church?" said the minister.

"O yes, sir; every Sabbath and two nights in the week, sir," responded the sweep.

"What church do you attend?" said the minister.

"O I always attend —— street! I was converted there twenty-two years ago, and I can never think of going anywhere else until I go to heaven."

The minister found, to his great surprise, that the poor chimney-sweep was a member of his own denomination, older in religion than himself, and apparently quite as likely to gain the Eternal City. The circumstance proves that we cannot safely judge concerning men's hearts, their hopes, joys, or prospects, by the texture of their garments or the lowliness of their occupation. Many whom the proud and gay habitually overlook, and consider as of trifling importance, as dwellers in the crevices of the earth, are nevertheless secluded gems, glittering in their appointed spheres, and will not be overlooked by the great Master of the universe when he comes to make up his jewels.

CHAPTER VIII.

VALUE OF THE DIAMOND.

EMS, like all other commodities in the market, experience the usual fluctuations of commerce. There never has been, and, from the nature of the case, never can be, an invariable value attached to a diamond. The general supply, the necessities of the merchant, and the fancy and ability of the purchaser, must ever regulate the price. One rule for estimating the value of the diamond has been to increase its value in proportion to the square of its weight. According to this theory, if a stone of one carat be worth twenty dollars, one of two carats would be worth eighty dollars, and one of a hundred carats would be valued at two hundred thousand dollars. Very large diamonds and fancy stones, that is, stones of decided color, such as blue, red, or green, are much sought after, and often bring fabulous prices. The Regent or

Pitt Diamond, which Napoleon I. wore in the
pommel of his sword, was once sold for over
half a million dollars, and is now valued at
much more.   The Braganza, an immense stone
from Brazil, and placed among the crown jewels
of Portugal, if a genuine diamond, (which many
doubt, and the Government will not allow it to
be examined,) is perhaps the largest and most
valuable stone in Europe.   It weighs in the
rough about eighteen hundred carats, and has
been estimated at twenty or thirty millions.

The diamond known as the Mattan, held by
the Rajah of Mattan, in Borneo, has been the
cause of a bloody war.   It is a stone of the first
quality, weighs three hundred and sixty-seven
carats, and in shape resembles a pear.   The
Dutch offered the Rajah two gunboats fully
armed and equipped, and two hundred and fifty
thousand dollars in specie for the stone, but he
refused to part with it, saying that on its possession depended the fortunes of his family.

Some have proposed to estimate the value
of soul-diamonds on the principle laid down
above—to *weigh* them instead of numbering,
and conclude according to their place in the
scale of fashion, politics, wealth, literature, or

religion. Great and decided successes they
regard as evidences of a great and valuable
soul, while the lack of brilliant achievements
they construe as resulting from the poverty or
worthlessness of one's nature. We once heard
a minister say that he very seriously questioned
whether all souls were alike valuable. We
thought the idea worthy of some reflection, and
carried it in mind for a considerable period.
Now whether all souls are alike valuable or not,
they certainly all sprang from a common source,
are all invested with similar capacities and re-
sponsibilities, have common wants, woes, and
dangers, and are amenable to the same tribu-
nal. While it cannot be shown that in the
comprehensive march of divine providence any
are overlooked or neglected, it is readily observed that, in many particulars at least, the
infinite Father has treated all with equal attention and love. True, all do not dwell on the
same acre, nor fill the same office, nor wear the
same garments, nor subsist on the same food;
yet every sphere has its pleasures and advantages, and every portion of the globe its natural
luxuries and attractions, which upon the whole
are not very unevenly distributed. For the

comfort of the most feeble and benighted, as well as the enlightened, the Creator continues to compound the atmosphere, load the clouds with moisture, cover the earth with fruit and verdure, burnish the sun, and stud the heavens with orbs of brilliancy. Mines of wealth have been discovered in all latitudes, and the phenomena of the changing seasons, the clashing elements in the tornado, the cataract, and the volcano, with all the intricacies of nature and providence, may be studied by the inhabitants of every zone.

In the sublime scheme of human redemption the interests of all souls are considered with equal care, and the same beneficent provision is made for each. *Jesus Christ by the grace of God tasted death for every man,* and the good tidings of his wondrous work he has commanded us to carry into all the world, and publish to " every creature."

None of us are sufficiently informed to decide certainly as to what is the most important or valuable quality of mind. All the works of Omnipotence are marked by variety, and Infinite Wisdom has found place and scope for every kind and grade of ability. The stars

are not all of the same magnitude, and there
is infinite variety of size and form running
through all the tribes of the lower animals, and
of the plants and minerals, yet who will tell us
which is most important? Man is too frequently
clannish, considering those unlike himself as
less useful, if not altogether worthless. Egotism
sometimes characterizes the cultivated special-
ist. His pursuit towers, in his opinion, above
those of all others. Some can scarcely perceive
why all are not mathematicians, or chemists, or
botanists, or linguists, or antiquarians, or his-
torians, or geologists. Others are disgusted
with theorizers, and have no patience with ab-
struse pursuits. They wonder why others are
not practical and useful ; why these men of
parts are not physicians, or lawyers, or teachers, or missionaries, or explorers, or statesmen,
or bankers, or merchants, or artists, or artisans,
or miners, or farmers. Why spend weary
nights and unrequited years over Greek roots,
fossils, or fine-spun theories ? The sordid,
purse-proud lord of mammon, consumed with
the passion of hoarded wealth, looks with inward scorn on the career of a colporteur, a
Bible-reader, or of one whose activities are gen-

erously spent in the promotion of education, benevolence, or religion. The zealous clergyman is to him a man with a large skull, but utterly void of any proper conception of his opportunities, who wastes in poverty the years which might have been turned to the amassing of money. The indolent and the voluptuous undervalue the industrious poor, whose toils provide their daily comforts. Silly notions of fashion and caste exclude some from the brighter fields of culture and comfort who are naturally in no sense inferior to those who exclude them. As in nature every animal, from the polyp to the king of the forests, has his sphere, so have all the lawful, though diversified, faculties and pursuits of the human mind. The Creator compasses the ends of his lofty administration in the employment of these multiplied diversities. Science needs men like Columbus, Kane, Newton, Franklin, Audubon, Agassiz, Darwin, and Hitchcock. Art advances under the direction of such minds as Palladio, Michael Angelo, Arkwright, Watt, Fulton, and Howe. Literature languishes without its Butlers, Macaulays, Milmans, its Miltons, Edwardses, and Irvings. Religion needs its Luthers, Wesleys, Howards,

Paysons, and Olins.   Law requires a Hale, a
Kent, a Marshall, and a M'Lean.   Government
needs a Wilberforce, a Pitt, a Washington, and
a Gladstone.   Now all these characters moved
in different spheres, and exhibited different talents, tastes, and temperaments ; yet who will
tell us which was most useful, whose soul was
most valuable, and whose least important ?

And if the soul of the reader or of any other
person has not yet evinced any very striking
qualities, it is far too early for us to conclude
that it is of any less importance than the noblest intellect that has graced the world.   In
the fourth chapter of this volume we have presented a multitude of examples in which dull
children developed into brilliant individuals.
These were plants that " flowered late," some
awaking to sterling thoughtfulness in advanced
life ; but suppose through lack of favoring opportunities, healthy stimulus, or from some
physical imperfection, one remains through life
in mediocrity, or even far below it, there is still
no evidence but that in the ages to come it
may tower among those whom we now regard
as the most gifted and brilliant.   These quick-
ening, adventitious circumstances of time can

only advance the most enlightened about half a century beyond the benighted, leaving all eternity to develop those who have not forfeited the exalting favor of the world's Redeemer. Every soul is invested in some degree with these six faculties : perception, reflection, memory, conscience, will, and affection. Now as every faculty is capable of eternal development, and every soul has started on a race so endless and wonderful, though some appear to-day to be loitering, it is far too soon to predict as to which shall attain to the most lofty achievements, or which is to be of least use to the Creator or the creature. This immortal jewel, like the natural diamond, is not to be valued chiefly for what it has done, but for what it intrinsically is.

The real value of the soul is evinced in the unflagging energy of its nature. The mind is so essentially active that from the point of its creation it probably never for one moment ceases in its interminable and ever-enlarging activities. Early in its career it becomes absorbed in some pursuit, which it follows amid varying fortunes with a persistence that exhibits the native sublimity of its being. This un-

bounded energy marks its career in every grade .
and sphere of human life. The persistent struggles of the most menial laborer disclose the glimmerings of human greatness. With him life is
a daily fact of toil and suffering, illuminated by
no promise of ease or elevation. Having long
since abandoned hope of improving his condition, conscious that life must become more and
more a burden, toil a more galling necessity,
earth with its fading rays less attractive and
eternity more dreaded, still to his shovel or
hod he bravely clings with a grasp only re-
linquished with life itself. Occasionally one,
baffled, exhausted, disheartened, chooses strangling rather than life ; but this is the rare ex-
ception, as most prefer

"To brave the ills they have
Than fly to others that they know not of."

Take another view of man. He has scaled the
barriers leading to place, and sits enthroned in
power. Millions of subjects are at his feet, and
billions of wealth within his grasp. Here he is
intoxicated with wine, surfeited with luxuries and
with praise, and enervated with wasting pleasures.
But all these do not destroy the native energy
with which he is endowed. He studies to in-

184 Diamonds, Unpolished and Polished.

. crease his wealth, improve his court, to perpetuate his throne. He would fain annex the continent to his dominion, or conquer the world, and lies down at length to weep or die under defeats and misfortunes.

Is man a well-bred soldier, clad in the tinseled livery of an empire, studying the art of war, or marshaling his forces ; is he a banker, planning far-reaching schemes of finance ; a merchant, opening untrodden fields for his commerce ; or an advocate at the bar, the same indomitable energy is exhibited.

If his toils are in the world of letters this native greatness is still more brilliantly illustrated. Here reason, feeble and uncertain, is girded and quickened by discipline. Memory is schooled and taxed to the utmost. His imagination pries into the mysteries of all worlds, and weaves in dazzling drapery the facts and fictions of time and eternity. In the great world of literary thought how he plunges and soars ! By most protracted and patient collation and analysis he evolves science from the intricate and shattered plains of nature. He classifies all material substances from the foundation of the earth upward. He searches the dusky past, writes history from fossils, and, peering through the realms of immensity, marks the invisible track of comets and distant worlds. Forty years man bends his mind under the examination of a scientific problem, until wasted form and wrinkled brow succumb ; but his son or successor takes it up, and rests not until the mystery is solved.

The value of this jewel could be urged from its earthly prowess, and from the astonishing exhibitions of its genius. Though fallen and semi-deposed man, still counts himself the lord of creation, and unceasingly wrestles with the giant forces of nature. He seeks to control and utilize all material energies, and often changes the face of the surrounding country. He has revolutionized the vegetable products of a continent, recklessly pursued and blotted from the plains of nature entire species of animal existence, while every-where he has more or less invaded the original harmonies of nature. Often beaten by the lower animals and made the sport of the elements, he gathers skill in defeat for subsquent prowess and triumphs. The mammoth monster of the deep, sought out in his far distant retreat, and, pierced by his dart, seeks in vain to elude pursuit by plunging to cavernous depths ; while on land the lion, the rhinoceros, and the elephant crouch under his authority.   He searches the bowels of the earth for curiosities and treasure ; converts seas and rivers into highways for the sweep of his commerce ; outstrips the eagle in aerial voyages, and harnesses the lightning to his rushing car. If it be said that his triumphant march has been misdirected, and attended with as much evil as good, we would add that these perversions of his nature do not detract from its intrinsic value, but afford the more painful illustrations of its transcendent greatness, even in deepest bewilderment and guilt.

Who can contemplate the multiplied examples of invention and genius, thronging the track of man in all the world, without being impressed with the incalculable value of the soul ?   Its triumph over matter proves that it is essentially different from and above it.   The ten thousand inventions to save and cheapen human toil, from the spindle to the quartz-mill, and the cylinder-press to the silent stretch of the metallic cable spanning the great deep and made the track for electric-winged thought, display but in part the inventive skill of his fruitful intellect. Hundreds of thousands of models of inventions have been deposited in the patent-offices of enlightened nations, and yet each generation, as if standing on the shoulders of their predecessors, eclipse all who have gone before.

The value of the soul is also displayed in its power of hoarding ideas. The memory is a vast invisible book, whose pages contain in legible and indelible characters the records of every impression, thought, and action of which the soul has ever been cognizant. In the hurry of life many pages and whole chapters may lie unseen for years ; yet innumerable and well-attested examples prove that nothing is obliterated. By the power of association or contrast, by the indescribable workings of the mind in sleep, in periods of excitement or of sickness, and under the wonderful quickenings of the intellect experienced in drownings, and in other forms of approaching death, every link of the wondrous past has been swiftly examined. No distance of time or space, or of varied and multiplied studies or undertakings, has in any sense eclipsed or dimmed the record.

The great value of this jewel appears also in the enduring strength of its affection. The soul, in a manner we cannot describe, discerns and selects its kindred spirits, to whom it clings amid joys and woes, and upon whom it lavishes the wealth of its affection. Damon and Pythias, two citizens of ancient Syracuse, were so devoted to each other's interests that when Pythias was condemned to die by Dionysius the elder, Damon generously took his place, allowing his friend to go and adjust his business. On the day appointed for the execution Damon was led out to die, but Pythias arrived in time to bear his own penalty. Dionysius was so touched with these acts of constancy that he liberated both, and their names have come down to us as the synonym of exalted friendship. So closely were the souls of David and Jonathan knit together that all the bribes and threats of King Saul were unable to divide them.

This intelligent affection, which distinguishes man and elevates him above other tribes of creation, is not destroyed by earthly separations, by lapse of time, by misfortune or death. It clings with tenderness to the memory of the departed, and weeps at the grave which contains the moldering remains of buried love. The aborigines of America sent tidings to their deceased friends by the birds of the forest; and the kings of Dahomey to this day deliver important messages to a servant, charging him to convey them to their friends in the spirit-land, and to facilitate his progress cause him to be quickly beheaded.

Washington Irving clung to the memory of his gentle and accomplished Matilda Hoffman with all the ardor of a youthful lover for more than fifty years after her burial, admitting no others to her place in his affections; and when he expired, at nearly seventy-seven, there was found on a table near his bedside an old and well-worn copy of the Bible, containing her name on the fly-leaf written in a delicate lady's hand. This had been his daily companion through scores of years.

The intrinsic value of the soul is further evinced in its capacity for communion with the Eternal. All the tribes of animated existence enjoy the bounties so freely lavished upon them, but man only is capable of ascertaining the source whence they flow, of appreciating and communing with the infinite Giver. The human soul inquires persistently after God, and will not rest without some conceptions of a Deity and some form of devotion. If knowledge of the true God cannot be obtained, some invisible creation of the imagination, a shining orb, a reptile, or a graven image, is introduced. A few perverted minds only, ignoring the loftiest faculty of their beings, lose themselves in the labyrinths of atheism and deism, either denying a supreme Existence, or ridiculing all forms of worship. But these unceasingly suffer from this unnatural trammeling of their noblest aspirations; from the felt worthlessness of all earthly acquisitions, and the emptiness of unhallowed enjoyments. The human soul is a boiling caldron of emotion, affection, and desire, coupled with an energy so persistent as to disclose its natural relationship to Him who never slumbers, and who wearies not in the ceaseless sweep of his eternal activities. It can find rest and felicity only in the proper employment of its powers in harmony with and in the study of its great Original. And it is this capacity for entering into holy communion with the august, invisible Deity, which evinces similarity of nature and loftiness of desire, which is the key to ultimate destiny. This we pronounce the noblest faculty of the soul, and the surest mark of its transcendent value.

The exalted nature of the human soul is further displayed in its unfeigned and ceaseless longings for immortality. This instinctive love of life and dread of death, which has characterized alike the civilized and the barbarian in every age, the Creator has deeply implanted in the human soul. This his goodness would not have allowed if annihilation were our natural tendency. As far as we can judge, no other creature on earth has any fitness for immortality. The brute unquestionably has mind of a low order, which may be destined for immortality, but which apparently makes no progress in that direction. Every creature in the world, save man, appears to attain early the highest summit of its ambitions. The cattle graze on the hillsides, drink of the rivulet, and sleep in the shadow of the trees, and think of nothing beyond. They are not concerned about the past or the future. They think not of the stars that shine above them, nor of the nature of the earth beneath them, or of the glory of Him whose presence pervades immensity. The bee constructs its comb with mathematical precision at its first attempt, and evinces no additional skill or desire ever afterward. The instinct of the bird, displayed in its first nest, the selection of its food, and in its earliest song, receives no subsequent additions. The silk-worm spins its amount of silk, lays its egg, and dies, without the slightest discoverable aspiration for any thing beyond.

But all man's present attainments are simply beginnings, and stepping-stones to something higher. Those intellectual giants who are believed by the masses to have meddled with all knowledge, and to have compassed the whole realm of thought, are, in their own estimation, as yet, the merest pigmies, struggling everywhere with mysteries and obscurities, and but just beginning their education. The illustrious Newton near the close of life said, in substance, that however he might appear to others, to himself he seemed a mere school-boy, who had perchance picked up a few brighter pebbles than his playfellows, while before him were spread out the vast oceans of truth which he had not had time to explore. Though excelling others in examining the intricacies of nature, he found no resting-place or limit to the rising desires of his penetrating mind. It cannot be that the Infinite Creator has formed so transcendent a jewel for annihilation, or failed to provide the means by which it may yet attain to viewless heights of knowledge and purity. A thousand times better to have been born without eyes, and all the organs of sense, without speech, or thought, or desire, than to catch a ravishing glimpse of this wondrous universe, hear its melodies, taste its sweetness, become just enough acquainted with its splendors to excite inquiry and desire, and then be quenched in the blackened depths of eternal oblivion.

If the well-defined faculty of the brute points unmistakably to its destiny, what less can be conjectured from the nature of the human soul? If the bee, filling its hive with the nectar of plants, on which it subsists, sealing up the cells that contain its precious morsel, gives promise of endurance ; if the numerous water-sacks in the stomach of the camel promise supply when other creatures are exhausted in the desert ; if an opening between the auricles of the heart, which never closes, and which enables the rac-

13

coon and other animal tribes to live long periods without breath, gives promise that the
thriftless animal will survive the rigors of winter, and appear fresh and hale in the spring,
may not the grasping, towering desires of the
human soul, and its astonishing susceptibilities
and progress, be reckoned as evidences of its
immortality? If not, we may well inquire with
another, "Wherefore was light given to him
that is in misery—to a man whose way is hid,
and whom God hath hedged in?"

All man's progress in usefulness and in piety
is regarded by himself as humble beginnings,
and in no sense commensurate with his desires.
That remarkable philanthropist, John Howard,
traveled, before the days of rapid transit, more
than fifty thousand miles, and expended thirty
thousand pounds sterling in behalf of the suffering. In 1780 Edmund Burke paid this eloquent tribute to his services: "He has visited
all Europe—not to survey the sumptuousness
of palaces or the stateliness of temples; not to
make accurate measurement of the remains of
ancient grandeur, nor to form a scale of the
curiosity of modern art; not to collate medals
or collect manuscripts; but to dive into the

depths of dungeons, to plunge into the infec-
tions of hospitals ; to survey the mansions of
sorrow and pain ; to take the gauge and dimen-
sions of misery, depression, and contempt ; to
remember the forgotten ; to attend to the neglected ; to visit the forsaken ; and to compare
and collate the distresses of all men in all
countries." He died, at the age of sixty-four, in
the midst of a foreign tour in behalf of prison-
ers, counting his benevolent undertakings but
half completed.

George Whitefield crossed the Atlantic thirteen times, preached eighteen thousand sermons, or an average of ten per week during a
ministry of thirty-four years ; but his abundant
labors fell vastly behind his ambitions. His
last sermon, delivered in the open air to an
immense audience, called forth all the loftiest
energies of his being, and was continued for
two hours. That night he halted at Newbury-
port, Mass. Faint and weary, with candle in
hand, he started for bed ; but lo, the multitude,
hungering for the word of life, throng the yard,
and his benevolent nature responds in a touching exhortation, continued until the candle goes
out in its socket, after which his exhausted form

finds the couch, where it lies down to die—cut off in the midst of his laborious and unfinished career.

John Wesley in his eighty-eighth year, though he had already preached more than forty-two thousand times, flew over England like an angel of mercy with the everlasting Gospel to preach. That many thousands through his instrumentality had gained the immortal shores, and that scores of thousands were also on the way, did not in the least dampen his ardor for still greater usefulness.

Thomas Coke, whose labors in spreading Christianity, and whose zeal in organizing missions among the poor and benighted, have not been excelled since the days of Paul, after crossing the Atlantic at his own expense eighteen times, and exhausting a large fortune in projecting and supporting missions in the West Indies, in Africa, in Asia, in England, Wales, Ireland, and America, died in old age on the Indian Ocean at the head of a band of missionaries whom he had fitted out, at the personal expense of thirty thousand dollars, to carry the Gospel to the East Indies.

None of these successful and wonderful men

approximated the measure of their holy ambitions, and no good man ever has or ever can in the brief circuit of his worldly career.

And what we have just seen to be true in regard to his usefulness is also true respecting his attainments in piety. However deep, long-continued, and blessed the experience of the soul in the things of God ; however comforting the inward assurances, bright the visions, multiplied and complete the triumphs of the cleansed heart over evil ; in its loftiest devotions it still exclaims, " I shall be satisfied " *only* " when I awake with Thy likeness."

We have not undertaken in this chapter to exhibit the exact value of this wondrous jewel ; that is a problem no finite mind can solve. As well attempt to number the sand, name the stars, or enumerate the cycles of eternity.

Reader, among all the valuables of this wondrous world the human soul is pre-eminently the jewel of jewels, outweighing, outshining, *outliving* every other. We cannot contemplate its numerous exquisite, diversified, and ever enlarging faculties ; its astonishing progress in the present life, though beset with innumerable difficulties ; its essential suscepti-

bility to pleasure and woe ; its power of endurance and of memory ; its probable imma-
teriality and indestructibility ; its strength in
research and discovery, skill in invention, and
versatility in pursuits of usefulness ; its wealth
of affection, sublimity of thought, and ardor in
devotion ; the nature of its aspirations, the towering sweep of its ambitions and hopes, and
the stretch of its onward destination, without
being overwhelmed with amazement, only excelled in the contemplation of its peerless Original. The proper keeping and culture of this
gem, holding constantly in view its value, its
relationships, and its future, are matters of infinite moment. No paltry considerations of
money, of empty fame, of ease, or of fleshly
desire, should ever obscure a mind so richly
endowed, or turn it from the loftiest pursuits
of which it is capable. If the Rajah of Mattan
considered the possession of his diamond the
circumstance on which the fortunes of his family depended, in how much higher and more important sense does the infinite welfare of every
individual depend upon the proper keeping of
that jewel with which the Creator has so be-
nevolently endowed him ?

CHAPTER IX.

LOST DIAMONDS.

DIAMONDS of great value have often disappeared for a time, to the great dismay of those to whose keeping they were intrusted, and to the financial ruin of those who had invested large fortunes in their possession. The plunderings attendant upon war have made sad havoc in every age among the precious gems, and nearly all the most celebrated jewels have exchanged owners during such periods. The Orloff diamond, which has been set in the scepter of the Czar of Russia, is believed to have been used many years ago as one of the eyes of an idol in a Brahmin temple. It was stolen by a French priest who had served at the shrine of a Brahmin god. After passing through the markets it was purchased by the Crown of Russia for four hundred and fifty thousand roubles, a pension of twenty thousand roubles, and a patent of nobility.

The Florentine Brilliant was lost by the Duke of Burgundy at the battle of Granson. A Swiss soldier picked it up and sold it to a priest for one florin. After several transfers it fell into the hands of Pope Julius II, who gave it to the Austrian monarchy, where it is still retained. During the French Revolution a renowned blue diamond of great value disappeared, and has never since been heard from. It was probably concealed by one who perished in battle, or was lost by the plunderer before reaching a place of safety. Still, as the natural diamond possesses no more thought or sense than any other particle of matter, as its uses are so limited, and its value so entirely factitious, its loss cannot be pronounced a matter of transcendent importance.

But the loss of the soul, the real diamond, presents one of the most momentous considerations within the range of human thought. Man's perceptions are so deep and clear, his capacities so varied and wondrous, his duration so boundless, and his susceptibilities of disappointment and sorrow so acute and continued, that his ruin affords a spectacle of deepest sadness and commiseration. The carbonic

Laborers at Work in Colesberg Kopje, South Africa.

diamond has attracted great and continued attention. Numerous volumes describing its nature, history, and uses have at different periods been issued from the press. But the soul-diamond has, in every age, been the subject above all others to rack the minds of the thoughtful. Its origin, its nature, its relationships, its duties, dangers, and destiny, have been ever-recurring problems to fill the inquirer with absorbing and incessant solicitude. Man has been the problem of problems. And this is not unreasonable if, as one has said, " Each higher species in the scale of organized being involves in itself the perfections of all orders below it." Standing at the very apex of creation, man inherits in natural organism the perfections of universal nature around him, while in mental and moral endowments he is allied to the higher worlds of thought and power, and ultimately to the great Creator. His nature affords a manifest clue to his origin and destiny, independent of all other revelations. A being of such complete and complicated formation could not be of chance ; and the number, variety, brilliancy, and strength of his faculties disclose his lofty destination.

But one sad fact has darkened all time. Man is in ruin. And the evil which he has incurred and bears has been in some form communicated to the world in which he dwells, and to every tribe of creatures that inhabit this terrestrial sphere. While it is true that ingenuity and design mark the formation of all things down to the smallest animalcules or infusoria, it is also true that disorders deep and widespread have from time immemorial shocked the globe. While goodness and mercy beam forth every-where to gladden the face of nature, severity and judgment are by no means concealed. There is clearly an immense falling short of the highest perfection in all the departments of the world. Material nature, even, does not answer to her highest capabilities. The surface of the earth is to a great extent cursed with malaria and sterility, locked in frosts, or scorched with excessive heats, and is also rent with frightful chasms, and ridged with rocky and impassable mountains. Internal commotions with frightful upheavals, rocking sea and continent, deluge her plains and harbors. The rush of her inundations ; the awful bellow of her volcanoes, vomiting devastating rivers of blazing lava ; the appalling sweep of her tornadoes, plowing madly through sea and land ; the blaze and thunder of her aerial elements, proclaim unmistakably that material nature, though still robed in beauty and grandeur, is perverted and engulfed in a partial ruin.

In all this the principal sufferer is man. Born in weakness and sorrow, he is shrouded in uncertainty, hemmed in by circumstance, startled by ever-present dangers, preyed upon by disease, until his precarious existence terminates and he passes to a world unknown. Man is the completest ruin in the world. Notwithstanding the grandeur of his formation, the rush of his insatiable desires, the crowning dignity of his station, and the lofty sweep of his faculties, he is sadly collapsed, and only exhibits in these fitful flashes of genius and strength what he would and should be but is not. How completely he fails to answer the lofty purposes of his being ! Who supposes the sensitive fibers and nerves of his ingenious mechanism were formed chiefly for pain, or that his polished frame was invented to draw the ponderous cart or become food for the wild beast ? Were the faculties of his mind adjusted for internal conflicts, distraction, and fear? Was his heart designed to be the grand hot-bed of all moral mischief? Are the possession of acres or of minerals, the donning of gaudy plumage, or the strains of ephemeral adulation, the loftiest objects of his proper ambition? Nay, verily; this cannot be affirmed without violence to one's own understanding. The truth is, man has suffered a collapse which has so inverted his high-wrought faculties as to render him his own worst enemy. His heart produces bitterness instead of love, his mind imbibes error instead of truth, his eye gathers darkness instead of light, his tongue utters falsehood instead of fact, his efforts result in sorrow instead of joy. Providences, circumstances, and toils ultimate in disadvantage, because of his native incapacity to turn them to their best account.

This moral ruin in the race is not only world-wide and universal, but has been frankly acknowledged by the wise of all ages and countries. The learned heathen of antiquity recognized the fact, and groaned under it as much as the Jews or the Christians. The Hindoo mother casting her child into the jaws of a crocodile on the bank of the Ganges ; the East Indiaman suspended on hooks in mid-air in violent self-torture ; and the wretched victim voluntarily crushed under the ponderous wheels of Juggernaut, confess thereby their ruin, and seek through these painful experiments a remedy they have long desired.

But how great the dignity of man's nature in the midst of all his perversions ! Lapsed in morals, he still sees and at once hates and longs after the good. Crippled and obscured in mind, he would still be wise, though his powers chafe with inward and unnatural friction. Sunken in deepest poverty, he would still be rich, though his accumulations are of the most grotesque character. His being is a blaze kindled from the original fires of the universe, and however low it burns, still exhibits in its faintest flickerings some luster of its great Original.

The perversions of exalted genius, everywhere witnessed, present one of the saddest evidences that men are already lost in moral corruption, and refuse to recognize their higher possibilities. These perversions mark alike the career of the artisan, the statesman, the orator, and the student. How pride, avarice, and thirst of power have taxed the abilities of statesmen and monopolized the skill of the artisan in the invention of instruments of cruelty! Sunken beneath his true level in the scale of existence, man madly batters his head against all surroundings. Having lost the corn, he quarrels over the husk. Counting matter and brutes beneath him, he seeks an unnatural and unhallowed supremacy over his fellows. Strangely forgetting all ties of relationship, community of present interest, and of ultimate destiny, he wages violently exterminating war against his own kind, brutalizes millions, wastes the resources of continents, and invokes the torturing power of all the elements upon his antagonist, filling the air with groans, and drenching the soil with human gore. Under the weight of his ruthless hand stately forests have been changed into arid deserts, the devastating waters of deep rivers spread over alluvial plains ; while cities and towns, the toil and pride of generations, have been swept with the besom of destruction.

The loftiest developments of literary application and genius have also too often been marred with great moral delinquencies. Indeed, persons of most abandoned principles, the completest wrecks in the entire shoals of humanity, have by their indomitable persistence towered in the sphere of letters, and shone like fallen but dazzling Lucifers.

Voltaire, guilty of great laxity in morals, was still the acknowledged "author-king" of his century, and with a power of wit and sarcasm never equaled could ridicule the deepest solemnities of time and eternity; like a rocket, blazing and dazzling all to the last, though its very brilliancy involved its ruin.

Lord Byron was a most transcendent poetic genius, a brilliant diamond of the rarest cut. Robert Pollok pays the following graphic tribute to his exalted talent, describes his genius and his melancholy end :

> "Others, though great,
> Beneath their argument seemed struggling, whiles
> He, from above descending, stooped to touch
> The loftiest thought; and proudly stooped, as though
> It scarce deserved his verse.
> He laid his hand 'upon the Ocean's mane,'
> And played familiar with his hoary locks;
> Stood on the Alps, stood on the Apennines,
> And with the thunder talked, as friend to friend,
> And wove his garland of the lightning's wing.
> Great man ! the nations gazed, and wondered much,
> And praised ! and many called his evil good.
> Wits wrote in favor of his wickedness,
> And kings to do him honor took delight.

Thus, full of titles, flattery, honor, fame,
Beyond desire, beyond ambition full,
He died! He died of what? Of wretchedness;
Drank every cup of joy, heard every trump
Of fame, drank early, deeply drank, drank draughts
That common millions might have quenched;
Then died of thirst, because there was no more to drink."

The celebrated poem "Beautiful Snow," which has been universally admired on two continents, and which the "London Spectator" pronounced "the finest American poem ever written," but concerning the authorship of which there have been many theories, sets forth in most touching utterances the plunge of a beautiful and gifted woman into crime and woe. If written by herself, as some have affirmed and others denied, it may be regarded as the last wail of a self-ruined soul still towering in lofty genius, though overwhelmed in the vortex of moral ruin.* We select two stanzas :

"Once I was fair as the beautiful snow,
With an eye like its crystal, a heart like its glow;
Once I was loved for my innocent grace,
Flattered and sought for the charms of my face.
       Father,
             Mother,
                   Sisters, all,
God and myself, I have lost by my fall;

---

* The authorship of this is now claimed by J. W. Watson.

And the veriest wretch that goes shivering by
Will make a wide swoop lest I wander too nigh;
For of all that is on or about me, I know
There's nothing that's pure but the beautiful snow.

"Once I was pure as the snow—but I fell!
Fell, like the snow-flake, from heaven to hell;
Fell to be trampled as filth in the street;
Fell to be scoffed, to be spit on, and beat;
    Pleading,
        Cursing,
            Dreading to die,
Selling my soul to whoever will buy;
Dealing in shame for a morsel of bread,
Hating the living and cursing the dead:
Merciful God! have I fallen so low?
And yet I was once like the beautiful snow."

English history presents the example of Eugene Aram, born in Yorkshire in 1704, and executed in 1759. This man, rising from extremest poverty at a period when schools and books were not easy of access, by dint of personal energy attained to deep and extensive scholarship. Maintaining his household by daily toil, he still so redeemed time as to secure considerable attainments in natural science, and render himself familiar with at least nine languages. At the age of fifty-five, while compiling a comparative lexicon of the English, Latin, Greek, Hebrew, and Celtic languages, he was arrested on the discovery of the skeleton of a victim

14

he had plundered and murdered fourteen years previously. Rejecting all legal counsel, he conducted his own brilliant but unsuccessful defense in a cool, scholarly, and ingenious plea worthy of the head and heart of a fallen angel.

No less striking was the career of the late Edward H. Ruloff, of our own country, executed at Binghamton May 18, 1871. One can scarcely tell whether he is more appalled with the magnitude and enormity of his crimes, or astonished with the powers of his grasping intellect. With no unusual facilities for culture, if reports may be credited, he made himself almost an adept in chemistry, philosophy, mineralogy, anatomy, zoology, criminal law, and mechanics ; and besides mastering the English, the Latin, the Greek, the Hebrew, the French, and the German languages, he is said to have been tolerably familiar with several others. To secure means to pursue his studies and to gratify other desires, he scrupled in the use of no expedients, and appears to have for many years divided his time between the most painful literary application and expeditions of plunder and crime. This villainous intellectual anomaly, confined in a damp cell, with gallows and

grave but a step in advance, by the faint rays
of a flickering taper pursued his studies in
philology to the last, as if no other thought
could enter his mind.

We cannot contemplate the career of these
dazzling intellects without feeling chagrined
that human nature, so richly endowed, should
sink so low. By neglecting the methods divinely provided for their moral recovery they
tarnished their opulent natures, and so eclipsed
the rising splendors of their being that, with
all their abilities and culture, they sunk in
darkness and sorrow, *unpolished* and self-ruined
diamonds.

Reader, you may treat with disdain the con-
nection between Calvary and the moral transformation of the human mind, you may count
yourself quite above the weaknesses of religion,
or consider yourself sufficiently brave to endure
whatever of ill eternity may unfold ; yet all
your cavils cannot dissolve or lessen your obligations to your Maker and yourself. You are
solemnly treading the slippery glacier which is
every-where skirted with frightful chasms.
Others as gifted and brave as you have died
in confusion and woe. Can you be indifferent

to the dangers of stranding your noble bark on the blackened reefs of sin, that every-where crop out through the billows of time? All human experience proves that the Infinite Ruler has connected happiness with moral excellence. There is no loss, no disgrace, and there can be no danger, in intelligent devotion to the law and the service of the true God. Learning, honors, riches, and happiness have crowned the pious in every age. The eternal destiny of your soul is a matter more transcendently important than any finite thought can conceive or numbers estimate. The culture and keeping of this priceless jewel have been committed to you, and upon you has been laid a fearful responsibility, from which you can never be relieved. If after a brief career you plunge from this gay world into a dungeon of gloom, and find yourself hopelessly lost, and far below all schemes of elevation and joy, how dreadful will be your consternation! You may pretend indifference to your moral condition now, but the final loss of the soul will be a calamity to which you cannot remain insensible.

The human soul is astonishingly sensitive.

It cannot remain indifferent to its condition ;
it cannot be satisfied without progress ; it cannot be indifferent to the opinions of others.
The mere thoughts of others, we might suppose, would be man's smallest concern, and yet
we do know that in a thousand instances they
have rankled in his bosom and poisoned the
streams of his life. Some have sickened and
died under a sense of ill-founded suspicion, and
others have died in despair on the discovery of
their sins. While writing this chapter we are
furnished with a striking example. Judge
M'Cunn, of the Superior Court of New York,
in excellent health, was, for malfeasance in
office, deposed by the State Senate on July 2,
and on the 6th he suddenly expired, exclaim-
ing, " They have broken my heart ! " He
could not be indifferent to public opinion.

Some of the most gifted geniuses have so
smarted under the criticisms of their contemporaries that they have crept away from society
and died in the solitude of their embittered
mortification. Copernicus so dreaded popular
condemnation that after preparing a treatise on
the Revolution of the Heavenly Bodies, he concealed the manuscript thirty years. Linnæus,

the great Swedish naturalist, nearly perished of mortification under the mockery attending the publication of his work on botany. The illustrious Isaac Newton so dreaded the merciless criticisms of his generation that he refused to publish his favorite work on Chronology, though he had re-written it fifteen times. Des Cartes forsook France, his native land, and died in Stockholm ; and the philosophic Hume, who boasted of his equanimity, we are told by an English author was so deeply mortified with his apparent literary failures that he at one time contemplated changing his country and his name. The elder Robert Bruce, unable to brook the lack of appreciation to which his patriotic exertions were doomed, died of disappointed ambition. The death of Bishop Stillingfleet is said to have been hastened by Locke's confutation of his metaphysics. The poet Racine declared that the least adverse criticism, miserable as it might be, occasioned him more vexation than all the praise he received could give him pleasure. Now if man cannot bear the censures of nis fellow, how shall he endure the withering frowns of his Maker and his Judge ? If so deeply pained with the breath of the finite, how shall he bear up under the sweeping blasts of the Infinite? If disgrace before sinful man is so crushing, what must it be before the great God and his holy angels? If the failure of a literary performance is a perpetual mortification, what will be the failure of a lifetime—a moral probation —an undying existence? And if man never forgets or pardons his own sins, which result in his shame and sorrow, how terrible must be the self-torture of the lost spirit.

The greatness of man's nature and the depth of his eternal perils are also evinced by his wonderful power of endurance under the most acute sufferings. The ability to suffer is probably graduated by the tone and development of mind. While it is true that suffering exists among the lowest orders of sentient existence, it is also true that this capacity increases with every successive step as we rise in the scale of intellectual being.

Man's capacity for mental pleasure and pain, independent of physical conditions, lifts him immeasurably above the other tribes of creation. They are disturbed by physical contact only, but his anxieties extend beyond the antipodes. With perfect physical health and elastic spirits, he is shocked with intelligence from afar which turns him gray in a night, plunges him into convulsions, or produces instant death. This may be occasioned by joy, by grief, or by fear.

His power of mental endurance transcends all our conceptions. The elephant, the master of the plain, captured in full growth, and unable to brook his humiliating captivity, has been known to lie tamely down and die. Not so with man. He survives the wreck of fortune, the most touching dissolution of earthly ties ; the loss of country, fame, and of personal honor ; he lingers in dungeons, and otherwise drinks the cup of grief, and then escapes to rain fury upon his enemies. Intense and long-continued suffering may cause the will to blench and the whole soul to writhe, yet no power of the mind exhibits signs of decay. Mind may be locked in profoundest solitude for years, and then awake with all the vigor and freshness of youth. Man's mental powers are neither lost by inactivity nor exhausted by suffering. The maniac loaded with chains may shiver amid the damps of a gloomy dungeon for many years, until his voice is like the creaking of an iron door, but he is still a man. Irrational, it is true, but not one faculty is lost. His eyes still flash with intellectual fire, and his whole soul bristles with life. Examples of the greatest suffering must be sought among minds most rarely gifted and extensively cultivated. As the elephant can probably suffer beyond the lobster, so the high-toned and cultivated philosopher has not only a more delicately-wrought and sensitive physical organism, but is capable also of more exquisite mental pleasure and agony than the savage. Examples of excruciating physical sufferings among persons of rarest gifts and culture have not been wanting. Without the loss of mental vigor or fortitude, they have lingered years with leprosy, tumors, and devouring cancers, until the exhausted body has literary fallen to pieces.

But the sorrows of the soul are infinitely more distressing. These are the result of the deliberate abandonment of principle and the perversion of energies and opportunities for virtue and usefulness. A full sense of these appalling consequences seldom takes possession of the soul until near the close of life. Then

profligate and ruined man awakes to his perilous condition, to groan and writhe beneath a
burden quite intolerable, but from which there
is no relief. Then, stretched on a pallet of suffering, with sickness and sin, the two great enemies of soul and body, blending their fury upon
his sensitive and immortal nature, we catch an
affecting and never-to-be-forgotten view of the
greatness of this precious jewel even in its
deepest ruin. What sweeps of memory! what
flashes of piercing thought! what swellings of
desire! what appalling utterances! what wither-
ings regrets of the past! what frightful horrors
of the future! what evidences of mortal agony,
even after the limbs are paralyzed, the eye
dimmed, and the hand utterly helpless! As
the expiring sea-monster rends the surface of
the great deep, so the departing human soul is
mighty even in death. How sensible men then
become of the emptiness of honor, of the im-
potency of human might, and the poverty of
riches. Louis XI. of France lived long in
utter horror of death. His physician, acquainted with his weakness, had only to mention the
subject to obtain large sums of money to bribe
him to most skillful medical watchfulness and

treatment. He is said to have taken fifty-five thousand crowns from him in this manner in five months.

"Am I very sick?" said a profane man who for many years had "heaped up riches and wrath" like the dust, and wholly neglected the better possibilities of his being.

"You are quite sick, sir," said the physician, "and should prepare for the worst."

"Shall I never recover?" he continued, straining his eyes as if to read his fate in the countenance of his medical adviser, "cannot I live a week?"

On being informed that he would probably continue but a little longer in the world, he replied,

"Say not so; I will give you a hundred thousand dollars if you will prolong my life three days."

A few minutes after this he expired.

Philip III. of Spain was counted a very moral prince, but when his feet were chilled in the cold river of death, and he thought of the searching ordeal he was soon to undergo before the face of the Eternal, he exclaimed, "O would to God I had never reigned! O that those years I have spent in my kingdom I had lived a solitary life in the wilderness! O that I had lived a life alone with God! How much more secure should I now have died! What doth all my glory profit, but that I have so much the more torment in my death!"

As the damps of death gather upon the brow all previous fears and mental agonies are immensely augmented. Thomas Hobbes, the learned materialist, utterly recreant to all moral obligations, and denying the real existence of mind, was still tortured for years with distressing inward fear. His guilty conscience and terrified imagination converted every shadow into a black-handed demon. But his fears did not waste with his body. Long unable to sleep or live in the dark, he took his final plunge into the regions of the unknown, shrieking as he went, "More light, more light!" Beyond the reach of earthly tapers, his soul was quaking with remorseful fear when the sensations of the body upon which he had predicated intelligence had utterly vanished.

John Randolph, of Roanoke, one of our most gifted American statesmen, and who at one period of life had experienced an unspeakable joy in discharge of his moral obligations, disclosed in his dying hour the torture of his soul in that thrice repeated but never adequately explained word, " *Remorse ! Remorse ! Remorse !* " Who can compute the loss of such a jewel ?

The gifted Edward Young in his inimitable style has described the dying scene of the accomplished Altamont, supposed to have been a young English nobleman of high birth and fortune, but whose moral delinquencies and dissipation had destroyed the happiness of his wife, wasted the inheritance of his only son, and brought himself prematurely to the grave. Bewailing his follies, and sunken in frightful depths of despair, he made this touching utterance : " This body is all weakness and pain ; but my soul, as if stung up by torment to greater strength and spirit, is full powerful to reason, full mighty to suffer. And that which thus triumphs within the jaws of mortality is doubtless immortal. And as for a Deity," he adds, " nothing less than an Almighty could inflict what I feel. My soul, as my body, lies in ruins—in scattered fragments of broken thought. Remorse for the past throws my mind on the future; worse dread of the future throws it back on the past. I turn, and turn, and find no ray. Didst thou feel half the mountain that is on me thou wouldst struggle with the martyr for his stake, and thank God for the flame."

These examples open to our contemplation a phase in human existence appalling beyond all our ordinary conceptions. Life's golden opportunities and joys having vanished, a tide of evil pours its desolating torrent upon the mind, while a fathomless depth of woe is revealed in the human soul. Clinging to the outmost verge of time, amid the ruins of material nature, these gems of intellect betray no loss of power, but bewail in terms too expressive and touching for imitation the sad ruin of their moral nature. And who, in imagination only, can peer into the yawning chasm where lie beyond all hope the blasted wrecks of high-born sons, and know the despair of deathless souls which were designed for the spheres of unsullied existence; and though now hopelessly sunken and forever lost, are still "powerful to reason and mighty to suffer," without being overwhelmed with the immensity of the ruin?

CHAPTER X.

HOW TO PRESERVE JEWELS.

HE safety of articles of value, of invested rights, of privileges and liberties, is usually supposed to be guarded according to the magnitude of the interests involved. Things of trifling worth are provided with few safeguards, while others are considered of such transcendent value as to justify the employment of all lawful inventions for their security. The prerogatives, territory, and honor of the nations of Europe are considered matters of such great importance as to demand the perpetual drilling of hundreds of thousands of troops who shall be constantly ready to fight for their security.

In the eastern portion of London stand a group of ancient structures known as the Tower. Here in other days dwelt the royal family, with their chapel for worship, and their prison for political offenders. The locality is a world of itself, with a history stretching far back into the ages, whose chapters exhibit the varied records of inconstancy and ingratitude, the skulkings of cowardice, the pomp of ambition, the savage triumph of brute force, the miseries of fallen greatness and of blighted fame. In our day these structures have become the receptacles of curious armor, and of a variety of relics collected from all sources, which are so grouped as to illustrate nearly every age of English history. One section is known as the jewel-house, and contains the regalia, the coronation plate, and the principal scepters, crowns, and jewels of the monarch. These are matters of great curiosity to visitors, and their value is considered so immense that the greatest precautions are taken to perfect their security. The building itself is made as strong as possible to resist the arts of the treacherous and the force of the elements. The curiosities are placed in strong iron cases so closely barred that no hand can enter them, while the rooms and all their approaches are guarded night and day by an ample force of trusty armed men. In one of these strong iron cages, on a cushion of the richest velvet, lies the Koh-i-noor, glittering with beauty and fire.

We have all heard of the vaults recently constructed in New York for the safe keeping of valuables. Down deep in the earth, beneath immense structures, floors and ceilings are formed of vast granite blocks bolted together through their centers with large bars of wrought iron ; steel vaults with twenty-five courses of steel and iron welded and bolted together for walls and ceilings, and floors of immense steel plates ; iron chests, grated windows, gates of solid bronze ; iron doors with combination locks, guarded day and night by policemen and private watchmen. Here are deposited sheets and slips of paper stating that A. has purchased a plot of ground, . that B. has so many shares of rail road stock ; a stack of papers show that the Government owes D. half a million. Here are also rings and jewels, and rich plate and curiosities, deposited by those who are living abroad. How careful people are getting ! The money is nearly all held and handled by the banks. We are afraid to have it in our houses or our pockets. We buy and sell, and accomplish immense transactions, with checks, and

15

a variety of paper pledges, without handling a copper.

But while so much commendable forethought and money are expended for the security of our stocks and ornaments, there is too frequently a culpable indifference, even recklessness, in relation to the keeping of jewels infinitely more valuable. How many pay large sums annually to secure their property from losses by the elements and the robber, yet allow their souls and the souls of their children to be daily imperiled! Care and toil for security should be intensified according to the value of the object to be kept. For man to allow his soul or the souls of his offspring to be drugged with false doctrines, fretted by strange passions, inflated with vanity, or wasted with vices, is the most culpable and suicidal policy of which the mind is capable.

It is by no means the end of duty to provide for temporal comfort, or to dissipate the crudities of the intellect. It is a thousand times less criminal to endanger the title to an estate than the fitness for immortality. The soiling of a garment, or the wasting of an estate, may be atoned for or endured; but a poisoning of principles, which culminates in the abuse of talent, the waste of opportunities and of time, and the losses that belong to eternity, is a matter truly appalling. The soul of every human being is born to the greatest conceivable perils. Before that infant mind lie the indescribable depths of untried liberty and of changing principles. It must feel its way into the region of responsible selections, states of mind, associations and habits, that shall fashion and fill its eternity. The demands of its soul are immensely more pressing than those of the body. Food, raiment, shelter, the temporary ownership of mines, ships, or of acres, are but the trifling accidents of its existence, while on its moral purity depends its endless felicity. .Let no one conclude, then, that because he has amassed a fortune for his child, or assisted his brother to prosperous· business, that he has thereby filled the measure of his obligation, while their souls remain untouched by the sanctifying efficacy of religious truth. Kindness to the body and solicitude for the present are the merest mockeries of affection where the true culture of the soul and its eternity are forgotten.

But how are we to rescue and preserve these jewels? In the mind of the writer it is entirely clear that parents have vastly more to do with the keeping of their domestic jewels, and that their influence in the matter begins at a much earlier period than is usually supposed. Children unquestionably inherit many of the diseases, physical traits, and natural qualities of their parents, and where their ancestors have for successive generations pursued any given career, they derive from them a natural impulse in that direction, whether to good or evil, not easily changed. Habit long continued modifies the brain, and changes essentially the character, conduct, and destiny of a soul and of a family. If any doubt, let them study the history of families noted through three generations for their miserly pursuits, their licentiousness, dissipation, indolence, or pauperism. The same principle is manifested in the favorable developments witnessed in families long noted for their brilliant intellectuality or integrity, their industry or piety.

The groveling tendencies of the savage are inveterate, and will crop out for several generations after his enlightenment. The children of a king whose ancestors have long enjoyed the splendors of royalty have the thirst of government so deeply inwrought that they can scarcely sober their minds to any lower sphere. The children of life-long paupers and criminals as naturally tend to the pursuits of their fathers as do those of the watch-makers of Geneva, or of the diamond-cutters of Amsterdam. Where the molding example and will of the parent are added to these inherited tendencies, the child as naturally yields to the influence as does the clay to the molding hand of the potter. Dr. Bushnell has admirably presented this point in his lecture on " Organic Unity in the Family."

He says, " The child being under the law of the parents, they will keep him at work to execute their plans, or their sins, as the case may be ; and as they will seldom think of what they do or require, so he will seldom have any scruples concerning it. The property gained belongs to the family. They have a common interest, and every prejudice or animosity felt by the parents, the children are sure to feel even more intensely. They are all locked together in one cause—in common cares, hopes, offices, and duties for their honor and dishonor, their sustenance, their ambition ; all their ob-

jects are common.   So they are trained of
necessity to a kind of general working, or co-
operation, and, like stones rolled together in
some brook or eddy, they wear each other into
common shapes.   If the family subsist by plunder, then the infant is swaddled as a thief, the
child wears a thief's garments, and feeds the
growth of his body on stolen meat ; and, in due
time, he will have the trade upon him without
knowing that he has taken it up or when he
took it.   If the father is intemperate, the children must go on errands to procure his sup-
plies, lose the shame that might be their safety,
be immersed in the fumes of liquor in going
and coming, and why not rewarded by an occasional taste of what is so essential to the
enjoyment of life ?   If the family subsist in
idleness and beggary, then the children will be
trained to lie skillfully, and maintain their false
pretenses with a plausible effrontery ; all this
you will observe not as a sin but as a trade.
Whatever fire the fathers kindle, the children
are always found gathering the wood.   If the
father reads a sporting gazette on Sunday, the
family must help him find it.   If he writes letters of business on Sunday, the children must

carry them to the post-office. If the mother is a scandal-monger, she will make her children spies and eaves-droppers. If she directs her servant to say, at the door, that she is not at home, she will sometimes be overheard by her child.

"If she is ambitious that her children should excel in the display of finery and fashion, they must wear the show and grow up in the spirit of it. If her house is a den of disorder and filth, they must be at home in it. Fretfulness and ill-temper in the parents are provocations, and therefore somewhat more than command-ments to the same. The proper result will be a congenial assemblage in the house of petu-lance and ill-nature. The niggardly parsimony that quarrels with a child when asking for a book needful for his proficiency at school is teaching him that money is worth more than knowledge. If the parents are late risers the children must not disturb the house, but stay quiet, and take a lesson that is not to assist their energy and promptness in the future busi-ness of life. If they go to church but half of the day, they will not send their children the other half. If they never read the Bible, they will never teach it. If they laugh at religion, they will put a face upon it which will make their children justify the contempt they express. Without any design to that effect, all the actings of business, pleasure, and sin propagate themselves throughout the circle as the weights of a clock maintain the workings of the wheels. Where there is no effort to teach wrong, or thought of it, the house is yet a school of wrong, and the life of the house is only a practical drill in evil."

It is from the united force of these inherited tendencies and the all-swaying influence of home that heathenism perpetuates itself. So Mohammedan families rear only Mohammedans, cannibals only cannibals, and gypsies and paupers are continually perpetuating their own kind. Granting all that can be claimed for the power of individual choice, and of personal responsibility after the development of reason and conscience, still all history and observation prove that the best men sprang from the best stock, and the vilest from the most vile, the successive editions on either side of the line usually excelling the preceding.

And it is upon this law of inheritance and

this all-molding power of home culture that we base in part our hope of the better ages which are promised in Revelation. As the facilities and practices of intemperance, gambling, licentiousness, and other sinful indulgences pass away, and Christian principles and practices correspondingly deepen and multiply, the temptations to evil will be lessened, and the incentives to piety immensely augmented. Children reared by parents trained in life-long godliness, breathing the atmosphere of sanctity from birth to their launch into the realm of maturity, will tend more easily to thoughtfulness and purity. We do not believe that by any processes of education, or by any attainments in moral power on the part of parents, children will ever be born without innate sinful tendencies. The fact of inherited depravity is, and must through all time remain, universal, and we think children should not be so identified with the forms of religion as to be allowed to forget that they need the regenerating power of the Holy Spirit. Nevertheless we fully believe that from the live-long sanctification of the parent stock better physical and intellectual tendencies will be inherited, and with suitable home culture, and under the operations of the ever-present Spirit, the child will early come to a conscious experience of a God-given victory over the evil, and a heavenly triumph of the good in his own soul.

We are aware that the existence of any good qualities received through inheritance is rarely mentioned by orthodox ministers lest we should seem to ignore the doctrine of depravity ; but without ignoring it, may not something be said and done to multiply and strengthen tendencies that shall unite with the Spirit for the overthrow and removal of this depravity ? No one doubts but that human nature in nearly every instance is capable of still deeper perversions, both in body and mind, which powerfully strengthen its depravity. And can there be any absurdity in urging the converse of this undoubted proposition ? If the leper against his wishes bequeathes his infection to his child ; if the inebriate's offspring are cursed by his fatal weakness ; if the children of the miser, the voluptuary, the prize-fighter, and the sluggard, are simply duplicate editions of their parents ; yea, if the blind, the lunatic, and the deaf mute sometimes involuntarily transmit their infirmities to their posterity, may not Christian parents do something for the moral elevation of their children by the correct and early cultivation of their own natures ? If a line of ancestors have been sane the child will not be likely to inherit insanity, If children spring from families never addicted to dissipation they cannot inherit the appetite and disease of the drunkard, and are consequently free from that peculiar inward temptation, and are so much the more open to Christianity. The children of healthy and intellectual parents are more likely to be highly intellectual than those born of invalids or the demented.

Who has not seen examples of children of excellent parentage, who, before conversion, like the young Israelite, tried to outwardly keep the whole moral law, and when their faith finally accepted the atonement, and the original damage or virus of their moral nature was removed, seemed at once harmoniously formed throughout, and full-fledged for an exalted Christian career, with every faculty marshaled under the direction of divine grace ? Much of the completeness and conscientiousness that characterize their after years sprang from their well-formed natures, which also resulted from the triumph of grace in the hearts and lives of their parents. And who has not witnessed other examples where reason, conscience, and grace have asserted themselves and gained the supremacy, yet from an ill-formed and deeply perverted nature, mental or physical, there sprang up tendencies which compelled a life-long battle with the higher aspirations, and were a perpetual weakness and grief to the individual? Many persons try to be good, and are, yet are they so clogged by inherited family peculiarities, which are so essentially a part of themselves that they never discover them, that they are more a burden in retarding Christianity than a power in advancing it. Their parents were not careful in preserving jewels. If any of these later utterances find a melancholy response in the heart of the reader, whose conscience and reason are daily battling against perverted physical forces, let him find consolation in the assurance that his persevering faith will ultimate in personal triumph, and that his changed heart and corrected life will work a gradual improvement in his physical nature, and enable him to bequeath a higher type of humanity to posterity.

If any now affirm that our argument is nulli-
fied by the character and conduct of the children of clergymen, we answer that any widespread reputed prodigality among their children
is a baseless assumption. Clergymen usually
have fair opportunities for the intellectual and
moral training of their children, but smaller
facilities for their proper manual discipline.
More delinquencies by far occur among their
sons from this last mentioned and almost unavoidable defect than from all other sources
combined. Farmers, manufacturers, merchants,
bankers, lawyers, and physicians can train their
sons to their own occupation under their own
superintendency ; but the ministry is not a pro-
fession to be chosen or to be bequeathed a
child, but a calling so sacred that the man of
God dare not "lay hands suddenly" even on
his own son. The nature of a minister's studies
and labors separate him above all other men
from practical association with business, so that
when his sons enter upon this eventful arena it
is without the guiding presence of their natural
adviser. But with all this disadvantage the
sons of most clergymen succeed. A gentleman among the Presbyterians, laudably anxious

to ascertain whether there is any truth in the oft-repeated assertion that *ministers and deacons' children do not often walk in the footsteps of their fathers*, took pains to collect accurate statistics upon the subject, and made the following report: " In two hundred and forty-one families of ministers and deacons there were eleven hundred and sixty-four children over fifteen years of age. Of these children eight hundred and fourteen—more than three fourths — were hopefully pious, seven hundred and thirty-two had united with the Church, fifty-seven had entered the ministry, or were engaged in preparatory studies, and only fourteen were dissipated, about one half of whom only became so while residing with their parents. In twenty-seven of these families there were one hundred and twenty-three children, all of whom but seven were pious, seven of them were deacons, and fifteen were ministers. In fifty-six of those families there were two hundred and forty-nine children over fifteen years of age, and all were pious." To fill the world with such families would produce a complete moral revolution.

Dr. Sprague, in his "Annals of the Ameri·

can Pulpit," has added valuable testimony in the same direction. From the families of the one hundred ministers whose career he recorded had been raised up one hundred and ten ministers, and the remainder of their sons had for the most part risen to eminence in the professions, or were distinguished as merchants or scholars. The family names of daughters are lost in their matrimonial connections, but the qualities of their parents usually distinguish their lives, and the fact that they are the daughters of clergymen usually opens their way to the best society. Dr. Haven once said, "We will venture the opinion that three fourths of the great men of this nation are not over two degrees removed from clergymen's families, or from families strictly religious."

This undeniable fact of transmitted tendencies should be a powerful motive to deep and consistent godliness with every thoughtful philanthropist. We care little about empty theories, and have presented these considerations chiefly for their practical value ; and we are more anxious that these truths be pondered by the young than the old. The youth of the present will be the parents of the future, and

we would not have them ignorant of the fact
that the good or evil of their natures and lives
will be involuntarily communicated to others,
that others may sigh and writhe under the
evils they now encourage, or be prompted toward excellence by tendencies they are now
struggling to establish. The "keeping of the
heart with all diligence," and the ruling well of
the human spirit, are matters of infinitely more
than personal importance.

But the proper keeping of these jewels involves also a wise and sanctified culture, beginning at birth and stretching indefinitely onward.
The culture of a soul does not begin, as some
suppose, when it enters the school-room, but
when it first finds its place in its mother's
arms. Vastly more is accomplished in the
molding of disposition during the infantile
period, when children are so often given over
to the mercies of professional nurses, than is
ordinarily supposed. We think an anxious
mother may safely conclude that when her
child knows enough to cry from the sting of a
bee, the prick of a pin, the slamming of doors,
the loud words and tumults occasioned by
anger and strife, that it is sufficiently advanced

to feel the touch of tenderness and be improved by moral influences. From that period its genuine culture can only be neglected with the greatest peril.

It is one of the most unaccountable things in the world that so many well-meaning Christian mothers can coolly deliver these precious jewels into the hands of ignorant and often vicious persons, to be by them retained and molded, if not neglected or poisoned, during this plastic period. Ladies who would not trust the nurse for an hour with a diamond valued at a hundred dollars will commit to her keeping for years the body and soul of a precious child, whose value exceeds the stars, and whose ruin is a matter we instinctively shudder to contemplate.

Several years since we were called to conduct a funeral service in the upper part of the city of New York. During the service we observed a rosy-cheeked little girl in the room and thought there was something very unusual about her eyes. Before leaving the house a friend said, " Have you noticed this child ? she is perfectly blind." On inquiry we ascertained that when an infant she was given over to the care of the nurse, and by undue exposure to strong light her little eyes became inflamed. The family physician prepared a wash for them, but the stupid creature in attempting to administer it took the wrong vial, and poured vitriol into both eyes, extinguishing forever the light of day. Mothers will shudder, and even weep, as they read this touching incident from real life ; but, alas ! what is at this time transpiring in their own nurseries ? Who are giving the early touches to those plastic but hardening jewels they claim to love so fondly ? What of their manners, their morals, their religion ? It is idle and heartless to say, " There is no danger ; the child is too young to be injured if well fed and warmed." Assuredly the seed of the great hereafter, whether you will believe it or not, is being planted, and if a drop of vitriol can extinguish forever the light of day from a little eye not yet developed into strength ; if a discolored mote in the hardening crystal will mar its purity, and the rude handling of an egg result in a deformity, what endless damage may be done to a child ere one is aware of it ! Nothing but exact personal supervision can meet the measure of responsibility and of properly developed affection.

We once heard an eloquent lady say, in addressing an assemblage of children, that she "once had a beautiful little flower" in her family, "a sweet little girl," but that while she was absent on a tour in Europe her "flower faded and flew away." We were strongly prompted to add, that if, instead of spending her money and time in sight-seeing, she had stayed to keep and cultivate her flower, it might not have faded and flown away so early. The great Creator has placed it within the power of the mother, above all others, to polish and preserve these jewels, and no earthly loss is half so sad to a child as that of a wise Christian mother. Where a child is despised or neglected by its mother, the worst consequences almost invariably follow. What a magnificent moral gem might not Lord Byron have been had his mother been as pious, sweet-tempered, and generous as she was gifted ! The bitterest thought of his brilliant but vicious and sorrowful life was, that his mother, who should have soothed, subdued, and elevated him, called him a "lame brat," and never loved him. Seed sown in the fresh soil of childhood seldom fails of its root and its fruit. Nearly all the melancholy examples of human wretchedness and vice that darken the world may be traced to the ignorance or recklessness of parents.

To save the jewels that glitter every-where around us, Christ Jesus must be enthroned in our hearts and in our homes. We must personally seek for purity and moral power. The day of emptiness and of affectation in our religion must end ; we must with our hearts believe what we teach, and really be what we wish to appear. It is not enough to desire the good of our children, our kindred, and neighbors. None will admit that they seek the ruin of their children or associates. But the case requires more than empty wishes, neutralized by indifference or a life of open sin.

And there are too many defects in our personal piety, and consequently in our example and government, for our largest success either at home or abroad. Outside glosses cannot long deceive, nor inside defects be concealed. Even our little children read and know us, as we scarcely understand ourselves. Our precepts go no further than our example, and our prayers no further than our faith. One may talk well, but neutralize all he says by covertly leaning in the opposite direction. There are vastly too many defects in some good families for the safe keeping of jewels. In one, otherwise well ordered, there is an undue thirst for wealth. Lucrative situations for their sons are sought and obtained without any nice regard or fear of the strain that shall be brought upon their principles. They are suddenly launched into the depths of a great city, surrounded with its multitudinous temptations and perils, as if their principles were too firmly established to be affected. How logical for such youth to conclude that their parents consider wealth first, and other matters of importance afterward. The vanities of style, caste, and ambition, in too many circles professedly religious, neutralize every thing said about virtue and right, and greatly strengthen and build up depravity. Going away to school when facilities quite as good are at home, where under parental oversight studies might have been pursued, has ruined not a few. Many professedly Christian families have no established religious habits. They have no prayer, no religious conversation or study. Religion with them is a name, an affectation, a garment to be worn on Sundays, at funerals, and when the parson calls. Can the rill in such a family rise above the fountain ? In other families every thing pertaining to religion is rigid, solemn, formal, and cold. The doctrines may be sound, and the regulations faultless, but the utter absence of simplicity, sweetness, and joyfulness repels instead of attracting the heart. Censoriousness makes a desert of many otherwise fruitful hearts, parching the soil where it goes. This evil usually springs from pride of intellect and want of sympathy and charity. But parents cannot quarrel with the Bible or its institutions without sadly demoralizing themselves and their families. If the parents live on "sour grapes, the children's teeth will be set on edge." Some fathers collect their children and pray upward in the morning, but unfortunately live downward until the evening. The long day, of course, overbalances the short morning. Some talk religion only to their children in tones of severity, quoting Scripture with fearful applications to punish their delinquencies. It is no wonder that boys go from the Sunday-

school to the House of Correction, and at last
die in the Penitentiary, when we consider that
the wisdom of those who trained them was so
much like foolishness. Our defective natures
mar our work at every corner and defeat our
purposes, and then we sit down and lament
that God "standeth afar off," and that his
promises are not fulfilled to us. "Train up a
child in the way it should go, and when it is old
it will not depart from it," is the pledge of the
Eternal, truthful and durable as his own peerless nature; and whatever discrepancy may
seem to occur between the promise and the
result can only arise from the defects in the
training. Failure results only from lack of
wisdom, of suitable tempers, and of effort. We
fail because we have not sufficiently understood
the nature of those jewels we have sought to
polish; we have been too lax or too rigid, too
formal, too bigoted, too fanatical, or have not
sufficiently attracted them by our love and
habitual sweetness. We have not dwelled in
God and filled our homes with the hallowed
perfume of heaven, or our children, perhaps,
would have been saved and ere this risen up
to call us blessed. O when shall we study

the art of polishing and preserving souls with the attention now bestowed on science, the fine arts, and the burnishing of the natural diamond ?

Finally, the preservation of these jewels can only be secured by infusing into their natures the principles and purity of Jesus. Granting that this in its completeness can only follow the cravings and faith of their own responsible individuality, we still insist that those cravings must be incited and nurtured by witnessing the examples and feeling the touches of purity around them. Advanced minds yet straying and wasting in their moral discolorment, must be sought out and plied unceasingly with all the wise and sanctified influences and arts of purified affection. Let us remember that while God has indisputably established the realm of individual liberty and responsibility, he has also so linked influence to character and destiny as to render each man, to a great extent, his brother's keeper and benefactor, and that the anxieties and toils of a lifetime are but a trifling outlay for the securing of a jewel so transcendently valuable. Every other pursuit or consideration dwindles into insignificance when compared with this manifest calling and obligation. Life's day is too brief, too perilous, and its possibilities too towering, to allow the thoughts to long dwell upon, or the affections to cling to, the vile or the ephemeral. Matters of magnitude and duration, infinitely outstretching man's conceptions, crowd his eternity, and press for his attention. Upon the humble efforts of the reader depend eternal consequences. Jewels will be either garnered or wasted, and the nature thus cultivated will be your ruin or salvation. Filled with such conceptions of existence and destiny, can any sacrifices be wanting to your usefulness, any labors a weariness, or trials a discomfort?

THE END.

Choice Books for Youth,

PUBLISHED BY NELSON & PHILLIPS,

805 BROADWAY, N. Y.

William the Taciturn.
Translated by J. P. LACROIX. From the French
of L. ABELOUS. Two Illustrations................ $1 25

Thomas Chalmers.
A Biographical Study. By JAMES DODD. Large
16mo.. 1 50

Word of God Opened.
By B. K. PEIRCE. Large 16mo................ 1 25

Christian Maiden.
Memorials of Eliza Hessel. With a Portrait. By
JOSHUA PRIESTLEY............................ 1 25

Stories and Pictures from Church History.
For Young People. Illustrated. Large 16mo.. 1 25

Agnes Morton's Trial,
And the Young Governess. By Mrs. E. N.
JANVIER. Large 16mo........................ 1 25

Life of Oliver Cromwell.
By CHARLES ADAMS, D.D. 16mo............. 1 25

Earth and its Wonders.
By CHARLES ADAMS, D.D. 16mo............. 1 25

Edith Vernon's Life - Work.
Large 16mo. Illustrated.................... 1 25

Exiles in Babylon.
By A. L. O. E. Illustrated.................. 1 25

Lindsay Lee and his Friends.
> A Story for the Time. Large 16mo............ $0 75

Gustavus Adolphus,
> The Hero of the Reformation. From the French of L. Abelous. By Mrs. C. A. LACROIX. Illustrated. Large 16mo........................   1 00

Heroine of the White Nile;
> Or, What a Woman Did and Dared. A Sketch of the Remarkable Travels and Experiences of Miss Alexandrine Tinné. By Prof. WILLIAM WELLS. Illustrated. Large 16mo............   1 00

Memoir of Washington Irving.
> With Selections from his Works, and Criticisms. By CHARLES ADAMS, D.D. Large 16mo........   1 25

Itinerant Side;
> Or, Pictures of Life in the Itinerancy. With Engravings....................................   1 00

Life of Dr. Samuel Johnson.
> By C. ADAMS, D.D. Large 16mo..............   1 50

Lady Huntingdon Portrayed.
> Including Brief Sketches of some of her Friends and Colaborers. By the Author of "The Missionary Teacher," "Sketches of Mission Life," etc.   1 25

Ministering Children.
> A Story showing how even a Child may be as a Ministering Angel of Love to the Poor and Sorrowful. Illustrated...........................   1 50

Lives made Sublime by Faith and Works.
> Large 16mo. Illustrated......................   1 25

My Sister Margaret.
> A Temperance Story. Four Illustrations. By Mrs. C. M. EDWARDS............. ....   1 25

Palissy the Potter;
> Or, the Huguenot, Artist, and Martyr. A True Narrative. By C. L. BRIGHTWELL. Illustrated.   1 25

Footprints of Roger Williams.
By Rev. Z. A. MUDGE. Large 16mo............ $1 25

Path of Life.
By D. WISE, D.D. Large 16mo............... 1 00
Gilt Edge...................... .... 1 30

The Ministry of Life.
By MARIA LOUISA CHARLESWORTH, Author of
"Ministering Children," etc. With Illustrations 1 25

Pleasant Pathways;
Or, Persuasives to Early Piety. By DANIEL
WISE, D.D. Steel Engravings................ 1 25

The Poet Preacher:
A Brief Memorial of Charles Wesley, the Eminent
Preacher and Poet. By CHARLES ADAMS. Illus-
trated...................................... 1 00

The Stony Road.
A Scottish Story from Real Life. Large 16mo.. 0 85

Pillars of Truth.
A Series of Sermons on the Decalogue. By E.
O HAVEN, D.D............................... 1 25

The Rainbow Side.
A Sequel to "The Itinerant." By Mrs. C. M.
EDWARDS. With Four Illustrations.......... 1 25

The Shepherd King;
Or, a Sick Minister's Lectures on the Shepherd
of Bethlehem, and the Blessing that followed
Them. By A. L. O. E., Authoress of the "Young
Pilgrim," "The Roby Family," etc. Illustrated. 1 25

Trials of an Inventor:
Life and Discoveries of Charles Goodyear. Large
16mo...................................... 1 25

Views from Plymouth Rock.
By Z. A. MUDGE. With Six Illustrations. Large
16mo...................................... 1 50

Words that Shook the World;

Or, Martin Luther his own Biographer. Being Pictures of the Great Reformer, sketched mainly from his own Sayings. By CHARLES ADAMS. Illustrated $1 25

Young Lady's Counselor.

By D. WISE, D.D. Large 16mo...............   1 00
Gilt Edge............. ....   1 20

Young Man's Counselor.

By D. WISE, D.D. Large 16mo...............   1 00
Gilt Edge....... ....   1 3C

Six Years in India.

By MR. HUMPHREYS........................   1 25

Young Shetlander and his Home.

Being a Biographical Sketch of Young Thomas Edmonston, the Naturalist, and an Interesting Account of the Shetland Islands. By B. K. PEIRCE, D.D. Illustrated. Large 16mo......   1 25

Children of Lake Huron;

Or, the Cousins at Cloverley. 16mo...........   1 25

Dora Hamilton ;

Or, Sunshine and Shadow. Six Illustrations. 16mo.......................................   0 90

Discipline of Alice Lee.

A Truthful Temperance Story. Illustrated. 16mo.......................................   1 00

Suzanna De L'Orme.

A Story of Huguenot Times. Large 16mo...   1 25

The Christian Statesman.

A Portraiture of Sir Thomas Fowell Buxton. By Z. A. MUDGE........................   1 25

The Forest Boy.

A Sketch of the Life of Abraham Lincoln. By Z. A. MUDGE. Large 16mo 1 25

AUNT GRACIE'S LIBRARY.

Ten Volumes. In a Box. Price, $2 50.

Clara and her Cousins.	Jennette; or, the Great Mistake.
Little Boarding-School Girls.	Old Merritt.
Our Birthday Trip.	Happy Christmas.
Little Annie.	City of Palms.
Mary, Anna, and Nina.	Stories About the Bible.

THE BOOKS OF BLESSING.

Eight Volumes. 18mo. *In a Box. Price,* $4 00.

The Little Black Hen.	The Prince in Disguise.
The Two School Girls.	The Carpenter's House.
Martha's Hymn.	The Rose in the Desert.
Gertrude and her Cat.	Althea.

COUSIN ANNA'S LIBRARY.

Eight Volumes. 18mo. *In a Box. Price,* $2 50.

Tom, the Oyster Boy.	Coney and Andy.
My First Sunday-School.	Freddy's Fifth Birthday
Willie and Clara.	Two Boys Side by Side.
Sunday Evening Readings.	Harry Perry.

AUNT HATTIE'S STORIES
FOR THE LITTLE FOLKS AT HOME.
Ten Volumes. In a Box. Price, $2 50.

Henry Maynard's Account-Book; or, What I Owe Papa and Mamma
Henry Maynard's "Book of Thanks;" or, What I Owe God.
Henry Maynard trying to get out of Debt.
The Little Captain; or, Ruling One's Own Spirit.
Our Looking-Glasses.
Hattie Hale's Likeness, and What it Taught Her.
Cousin Robert's Story.
Katie and the Cup of Cold Water.
Work and No Work.
Constance and Carlie; or, "Faithful in that which is Least."

THE WILLIE BOOKS.

Five Volumes. 18mo. *In a Box. Price,* $3 00.

Willie's Lessons.	Willie Trying to be Thorough.
Willie Trying to be Manly.	Willie Wishing to be Useful.
	Willie Seeking to be a Christian.

GLEN ELDER BOOKS.

Five Volumes. In a Box. Price, $6 00.

The Orphans of Glen Elder. The Lyceum Boys.
Francis Leslie. The Harleys of Chelsea Place.
Rosa Lindesay.

LIBRARY FOR LITTLE LADS AND LASSES.

Five Volumes. In a Box. Price, $3 00.

Archie and his Sisters. Stories about the Little Ones.
Archie and Nep. More Stories about the Little Ones.
The Fisher Boy's Secret.

LYNTONVILLE LIBRARY.

Four Volumes. In a Box. Price, $4 50.

Life in Lyntonville. Fishers of Derby Haven.
Miss Carrol's School. Grace's Visit.

LOVING HEART AND HELPING HAND LIBRARY

Five Volumes. In a Box. Price, $5 50.

Nettie and her Friends. An Orphan's Story.
Philip Moore, the Sculptor. Carrie Williams and her Scholars.
The Story of a Moss-Rose.

WINIFRED LEIGH LIBRARY.

Four Volumes. In a Box. Price, $4 00.

Winifred Leigh. In Self and Out of Self.
The Captive Boy in Terra Del Fuego. Hetty Porter.

LITTLE DOOR-KEEPER LIBRAhY.

Five Volumes. In a Box. Price, $6 00.

Little Door-Keeper. Captain Christie's Granddaughter.
Miracles of Heavenly Love in False Shame.
Daily Life. Joe Witless.

MAUDE GRENVILLE LIBRARY.

Five Volumes. In a Box. Price, $6 00.

Maude Grenville. Enoch Roden's Training.
Heroism of Boyhood. Victor and Hilaria.
The Children of the Great King.

www.ingramcontent.com/pod-product-compliance
Lightning Source LLC
Chambersburg PA
CBHW020054030726
47498CB00006B/1775